In this issue of *Fantasy Tales* you will discover:
'*Now and Again in Summer*' by award-winning novelist Charles L. Grant tells of a woman's terrifying train journey into fear.

In Lin Carter's '*The Thievery of Yish*', a hapless thief burgles the home of a master magician and suffers the diabolical consequences.

Supernatural troubleshooter Sabat is lured into a nightmarish trap by the revenge-seeking undead in Guy N. Smith's '*Vampire Village*'.

A chance encounter on the road leads to terror in C. Bruce Hunter's '*The Farmer and the Travelling Salesman's Daughter*'.

Plus fiction and verse by Darrell Schweitzer, J.N. Williamson, David Riley, Robert E. Howard and others, illustrated by some of the genre's top artists, and *The Cauldron* featuring fantasy news and views.

"*A leading outler for contemporary horror and fantasy fiction*" — The Penguin Encyclopedia of Horror and the Supernatural

FANTASY
Tales

Vol. 10   No. 1

Published by
Robinson Publishing,
11 Shepherd House,
Shepherd Street,
London W1Y 7LD

Vol. 10
Issue No. 1
Autumn 1988

Editor: Stephen Jones
Associate Editor: David A. Sutton
Managing Editor: Annabel Edwards
Publisher: Nick Robinson

Editorial Correspondence

Manuscripts should be addressed to David A. Sutton,
194 Station Road, Kings Heath, Birmingham B14 7TE,
UK. All manuscripts are welcome but must be
accompanied by a stamped, self-addressed envelope or
they cannot be returned.

Artwork Correspondence

Examples of artwork should be addressed to Stephen
Jones, 130 Park View, Wembley, Middlesex HA9 6JU,
Uk. All examples of artwork are welcome but must be
accompanied by a stamped, self-addressed envelope or
they cannot be returned.

Subscriptions

Fantasy Tales is published twice a year. It is available
on subscription direct from the publishers at £3.60 for
4 issues in the UK (including postage and packing) and
£7.60 ($14.00) by airmail overseas. Subscription
enquiries should be addressed to Subscription Dept.,
Robinson Publishing, 11 Shepherd House, Shepherd
Street, London W1Y 7LD, UK.

Advertising

Enquiries should be addressed to Advertising Dept.,
Robinson Publishing, 11 Shepherd House, Shepherd
Street, London W1Y 7LD, UK.

Copyright

ISBN 0 948164 85 9
Typeset by Grassroots, London N3 2LJ
Printed by Wm. Collins & Sons Ltd., Glasgow

CONTENTS

CHARLES L. GRANT   Now and Again in Summer   1
The train's destination was a nightmare!

LIN CARTER   The Thievery of Yish   11
Even the best thief knows not to steal from a magician.

GUY N. SMITH   Vampire Village   16
The undead snare Sabat in a diabolical trap.

C. BRUCE HUNTER   The Farmer and the travelling   29
                 Salesman's Daughter
A chance encounter on the road leads to terror.

J.N. WILLIAMSON   Fancy That   37
True love even transcends the physical universe.

CHRIS MORGAN   Touching   43
In her dreams she enjoyed watching her husband die.

DARRELL SCHWEITZER   A Vision of Rembathene   53
A king must look upon the face of a god to save a city.

DAVID RILEY   Writer's Cramp   64
Only he could see the withered hand that cursed him.

CHRIS NAYLOR   The Cloven Cross   83
Verse.

ROBERT E. HOWARD   Memories   84
Verse.

THE CAULDRON   85
*News from the fantasy field, profile of Chris Achilleos
and readers' letters.*

STEPHEN KING

The Man in Black fled across the desert, and the Gunslinger followed...

THE DARK TOWER

VOLUME 1: THE GUNSLINGER

HIS NEW EPIC FANTASY—

Out now in Sphere paperback

SPHERE

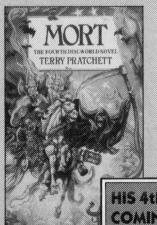

The hills darkened and the wind whispered and the sky broke out in stars when the light at last failed. (Artist: Lynne Taylor)

NOW AND AGAIN IN SUMMER

Charles L. Grant

The silence: like the hush of a grey morning after the season's first snowfall, or the quiet, the long and dark quiet just after twilight, in a graveyard where the flowers in cracked vases are brittle and brown; the sound of the fog; the voice of a shadow; the protection of the draperies drawn over the locked window, muffling traffic and wind and footsteps on the pavement.

The silence

She rolled over and held her breath, listening.

that whispered

She opened her eyes and held her breath, staring.

you're alone all alone

Your imagination, Joan, she told herself as her arms grew rigid at her sides and the soles of her bare feet began a soft annoying tingling; it's your imagination.

Listening.

Staring.

Finally sitting up and switching on the bedside lamp in one hurried move, blinking away the glow to search the room without climbing from the bed.

She smiled and shook her head.

The wardrobe doors were still tightly closed, the basin under the mirror wasn't filling with things crawling to get her, the table and chair against the opposite wall hadn't been turned upside down. There were packages on the floor, books stacked on the vanity; the room's only armchair was still set by the window.

Everything was where it should be; nothing had been moved.

And outside, two floors below, the guttering roar of taxi cabs, the rumble of trucks, a group of pedestrians whose heels sounded like horses.

The world hadn't gone away; it was all still there.

A ghost of anxiety made her yawn, receding echoes of an empty nightmare had her checking the room one more time, but the clock on the night table finally forced her out of bed, and she stretched, touched her toes, rolled her shoulders, pushed her fingers back through long brown hair that reached down to her waist. Another yawn that popped her jaw as she opened the door a crack and peered down the narrow hall to see if the other guests were stirring; closing it again and stripping off her nightgown, slipping into her robe, grabbing up a small bag that held her makeup, and all her brushes.

She grinned, almost giggled; I'm a convict, she thought, making a break for the wall.

A rush then into the bathroom before anyone could spot her, still not used to having to share sink and tub with people she didn't know, hardly passed two words with, and she especially couldn't let them see her before she dressed. Certainly not in the morning. The only time it had happened, two days after her arrival, she'd thought she would nearly blush herself to death.

Now she was more confident; the bed-and-breakfast almost felt like home.

Tomorrow, she told herself, I'm going to be naked and dare them to come.

The tub filled, steaming; the basin filled, sputtering; and she winked at her reflection in the spotty mirror. It was Saturday. No definite plans to fill the hours until dark. Nothing to do but hang around, play the tourist, maybe find a seat for a show.

A shrug—why not? Making schedules for herself was boring— and twenty minutes later she was down in the breakfast room, at a corner table by herself, munching a triangle of charred toast and avoiding the others, who never looked at her, never spoke to her beyond a brief morning's greeting marked with polite absent smiles.

And that was fine with her.

She didn't invite company, didn't want it, didn't need it.

She had come all the way to London as a test, to see if she was really and truly a grown-up after thirty-seven years; she had no idea what she would receive if she passed.

But she knew full well what she would get if she ran home too soon—a smug chorus from her friends of *I told you so, Joanie*.

Those same friends who seldom left the county when vacation time came around, and never left the country at all because the world was too big and, they claimed, too frightening, too cold. There were terrorists, airplane crashes, rapists in every nation just waiting for foreign victims, and why would she want to give up a sure thing at home for something so filled with the uncertain and the unknown?

There be dragons? Joan had asked, and they hadn't understood.

She, on the other hand, had gone to college; she had even once been married. And when at last the television commercials had done their job, made their promises, she was determined that she might even learn what romance had to offer.

A grin as she finished her tea.

Romance. That's what she told her friends because that's what they wanted to hear. What she really meant, however, was adventure—which was, at the last, just something different than what she had, and no longer wanted. And so far, the adventure had consisted of taking the tours and listening to the guides and falling in love with everything she'd ever seen in the movies, read in her books, dreamed of at night when she dreamt herself a queen.

Not great; not terrible; but no damned adventure.

She rose with a sigh, and lingered for a few minutes in the foyer reading the theatre notices and museum discounts pinned to a corkboard on the wall. Then she went outside, took a deep breath, and glanced up at the sky.

There was blue, there was sun, there were trees whose leaves dappled the pedestrians with shadow. A delivery van. A dog walking its owner. A park at the end of the block where flowers accented the green.

A breeze that had her hair tickle her nose, and she decided to walk. Nowhere in particular. Just walk, and look, and perhaps something would strike her fancy and give her a good day, something she could bring home to show that she hadn't hidden after all.

That's what they thought she would do, of course—hide among the other tourists, hide in the hotel, hide in the largest stores where she was no different than the others, and where she wouldn't be alone. They didn't credit her with enough courage to go into the small places, the dusty places at the bottoms of steps at the bottoms of narrow lanes, where she would be the only one browsing through the aisles; they certainly didn't believe she'd take in a night club, let a strange man hold her hand, let another stranger hold her dancing.

Her best friend had told her she was making a mistake, that she was, inside and out, a small town girl the city would eat alive; and London, for God's sake? Once off the plane she'd never be seen again.

Joan felt the heat in her cheeks then, the anger that never failed whenever she heard the warnings, the cautions, the well-meaning fears that were little more than insults. She ducked her head and shook it, raised it again and felt better. And an hour later, after window shopping and dodging traffic, she stood on a corner on Charing Cross Road where it struck her that maybe she ought to take her first train ride ever. It didn't matter where; it would be a true and honest adventure, her first time beyond the city and wouldn't they be amazed.

She nodded sharply.

She smiled sweetly at a glum young man in gleaming leather who collided with her as she wheeled about and fairly marched through the nearest Underground entrance. A moment at the map on the tiled wall, and she decided that Victoria Station was the place to go. Waterloo somehow had echoes she didn't trust.

And once at Victoria, bracing herself against the noise and the smells of food and all those people, she examined the dizzying lists of stops, puzzling at the times that didn't seem to make sense. She almost panicked. She breathed deeply. And finally, in exasperation because the adventure seemed to be dying, she reached out a finger and brushed a smudge of dirt away from a place called Kelworth Market.

It was the right place.

She knew it.

This was what she wanted. There were no historical or literary associations right to mind, nor did it appear that British Rail had made it a vital part of its schedule. A village perhaps, or even less than that.

No tourists.

Just her.

A flutter about her heart as she paid for the ticket.

A chill and hollow in her stomach as she hurried for the gate when she realized the time and feared she'd miss her train.

This is dumb, she thought as she rushed toward the front, dodging school children in uniform who paid her no mind; when you get there, you idiot, you're going to find out there's no train back until tomorrow and no place to stay.

She giggled.

A matron in foxfur glared over her glasses.

She hauled herself into the first car and immediately found a place to sit facing forward, pressed close to the window and rested her forearms on the table between her seat and the one facing.

Dumb, Joanie Ash, this is truly dumb.

A bit sheepishly she shrugged at her faint and fading reflection in the dust-stained window, and winked when the train began to pull away.

Last chance, she warned as she leaned back and closed her eyes; and before there was an answer, there was the voice of the wheels, the rocking, and sleep.

A long sleep, she realized when she blinked and sat up with a start, rubbed her eyes and damned the sun striking god knew how many hours past noon.

She yawned, and she stretched, and she raised herself off the seat to check the rest of the car. It was empty. And she heard nothing but the rocking and and the creaking and the wind. A frown as she sat again, wondering how many stops she'd missed, a hand rubbing at her throat when she wondered if she'd missed hers.

"Swell," she muttered. "Just . . . swell."

Outside there were hills, low and green, patched with trees, pocked with cattle, the near hedgerows a blur until the train began to slow with a shudder. There were no houses she could see, no road or signs—just a glint of water, and the deepening blue of a sky cut ragged at the horizon.

Nervously, she massaged the back of her neck and wished she had at least picked up one of the maps on sale at the London terminal. It would have at least given her an idea of how far she'd traveled, how far she had to go. Not that she was afraid, she hastened to assure the reflection that looked back at her, pale; this was, after all, an adventure, remember? And no one would ever accuse her of hiding again. Not now. Not when she was well and truly too far from her bed and books for them to offer comfort.

Slower now, brakes squealing, and a weathered concrete platform slid past the window, a bench with a capped old man dozing, two girls in tartan skirts waiting, a canted sign on a chipped stone wall she had to read twice before she realized she was here.

Kelworth Market.

In the middle of nowhere.

Count your blessings, she thought; the sun is out and there's no fog. Remember the fogs Dad used to tell you about, when he was in the army? Thick as soup, not as tasty, a man could fall into a hole and never be found kind of fog?

Right, she answered sourly as she stepped stiffly down onto the platform and put her hands on her hips; right. I'm counting, so what?

As far as she could tell, Kelworth Market was the stationhouse, the platform, and on the other side of the tracks a wind-weary wooden fence with more slats fallen than standing. There were no buildings, house or otherwise and, when she passed through the small waiting room to the platform on the other side, not a single road that she could see.

Nothing but the hills, and the sky, and the soft soughing wind.

"Damn," she said.

"Ladies oughtn't to swear," a hoarse voice said from her left.

She looked at the old man on the bench, who was looking back at her, his hands deep in his overcoat pockets, his face puffed where the wrinkles didn't sink it.

"Sorry," she said.

He shrugged with a tilt of his head. "No need. I know the feeling."

She smiled at him politely and walked away, to the platform's far end, where the tracks dodged around a curve overhung with heavy boughs. It must be a commuter station, she decided. The town itself is probably miles away, at least too far to walk to. Maybe over that hill, or the one over there. But when she looked again, hunting confirmation, there was no car park, no lights, and staring into the weeds on the other side of the rails failed to produce signs of a path that would mark where all the passengers come and go.

"Some adventure," she muttered, slipping one hand into a hip pocket as she returned inside to find a schedule.

"Mel," the old man said from the doorway. "Mel Tawlent."

She started, nearly jumped, and swallowed twice before she was able to give her name.

"American?"

"Yes."

He cleared his throat noisily and tugged at a faded blue scarf wrapped twice about his throat. "Teacher?"

"No. Just a tourist." Then she waved helplessly at the empty room. "A lost one, from the look of it. I can't even find a schedule."

After a disconcerting stare he cleared his throat and walked away, and frowning she followed, through the chilled shadow of the roof, into the not much warmer sunlight where he took his bench again and with effort crossed his legs. His baggy trousers were worn through at the cuffs, his shoes badly scuffed, and his colourless socks had rippled down to his ankles.

From an inside pocket he pulled a bar of chocolate, carefully ripped back the paper and offered her a share.

"No thanks," she said. "Are you . . . do you live here?"

"Not me, lass," he said with a quick laugh. "I ain't no bird, y'know. Can't live in trees."

She remembered then the girls in the tartan skirts, but they were nowhere in sight. After a moment's confusion, she supposed they must've boarded the train while she had disembarked, but if the old man—Mel?—didn't live here, why hadn't he gone as well, why hadn't he left?

A check of the sky told her she had only a couple of hours left before dusk, and if she didn't get herself in gear she'd have to share the bench with him, probably listen to war stories until the cows came home. Unless a train came along. Unless a knight happened by on a charger built for two.

Besides, she had to move, because standing there made her aware of the quiet. The silence. A breeze blowing without rustling the leaves, no creak of wood, no snap of her heels. There was no voice here, not like London, not like home; there was no voice at all to tell her she wasn't deaf.

Her fists clenched; the world is still here.

Her throat dried; you can see it, it's there.

And she pinched the back of her hand until she winced, and was sure she wasn't sleeping.

"Well, nice meeting you," she said brightly, and after a moment's indecision, decided to head west, toward the hills beckoning the sun.

"Where're you off to then?" he asked, twisting around to watch her.

"I don't know," she admitted. "A bed-and-breakfast, I suppose. A farmhouse. Wherever I can find a telephone to find out about the next train."

"Ain't one," Mel said, turning around again.

She stared at the back of his head. "Come again?"

"Ain't one."

"You mean I have to wait until tomorrow?"

He shook his head.

"Great." She glared at the waiting room, glared at the sky. "Well, I can't wait until Monday, for heaven's sake. Where will I sleep? I'll just have to—"

The man rose slowly, his coat falling in jerky stages until it covered his knees. And when he looked at her from beneath the soft brim of his cap, she took a step backward and nearly fell to the tracks.

"Ain't one, miss," he said again. "Not tomorrow, not Monday, nor Monday next if that's what you're thinking." He didn't smile. "You've come, and that's the end of it for a while." He saluted her with two knobby fingers. "Now if you'll pardon me, miss, I've walking to do. My bones are too old to be sitting so long."

She gaped, a nervous hand not quite clutching at her chest, watching as he paced the length of the platform and back. Again. A third time. Looking down, never speaking, in and out of shadow while his shoes squeaked and flapped.

Her first thought was *he's crazy*, and her second was to get the hell away before he attacked her, raped her, stole her money, vanished, and left her to die.

But when she turned again and saw the fields beyond the weeds, the hills beyond the fields, and the birds passing over, never circling, never calling, when she saw the leaves moving and didn't hear a sound, she knew he wasn't lying.

And she also knew it wasn't silence at all.

He passed her then in his exercise and said, "When you think about it, miss, it's rather exciting."

Her arm swung out viciously before she could stop it, but she missed him and lost her balance, fell and half jumped to the tracks where she felt the iron beneath her feet and began to run. Not fast. A slow trot. Conserving her energy. Writing postcards in her mind: *ladies, you'll never guess what happened to me*. Slowing when she found herself growing short of breath, turning to see how far she'd gone, and seeing the platform not a handful of yards distant.

"Tried it myself a few times," Mel said as he took the corners neatly. "Didn't get much farther, I can tell you. Waste of time, if you want to know. Better just to wait."

She ran.

She turned.

"It gets dark out there, miss. Mark me, it gets dark."

She turned.

She ran.

She stumbled and fell and lay her head on her wrist, one foot hooked over a rail, the other kicking softly the gravel beneath. In time there was a footstep, and a gentle hand on her arm. She considered resisting, and surrendered, letting the old man lead her back to the station, help her to the platform, guide her to the bench.

He sat on one end, she on the other.

The hills darkened and the wind whispered and the sky broke out in stars when the light at last failed.

"Those girls," she asked, staring at the place where she knew the tracks to be.

"Don't know." His voice, face unseen, was younger now and less grating. "They was here when I come. Never said a word to me, that's a fact. They was scared."

"So am I."

"And me."

She pushed her hair from her eyes. "But you didn't get on the train."

"Couldn't," he said. "My time'll come."

"And mine?" she asked, closing her eyes immediately his shoulders lifted in a shrug.

He tugged at his cap. "But it's an adventure, don't you think? You don't die, you don't starve. And now and again in summer someone comes along to chat."

The wind, slightly damp.

"You wait," she said.

"Aye."

"And wait."

"What else?"

And when the waiting ends, she wondered; when the waiting ends, where does the train take you next?

But she didn't ask.

She pulled her legs beneath her and folded her arms against the night.

And listened to the endless silence, to the endless absence of sound.

Charles L. Grant *is a prolific editor, short story writer and novelist. He sold his first story, 'The House of Evil', to* Fantasy & Science Fiction *in 1968. His books include* The Curse, The Hour of the Oxrun Dead, The Nestling, The Tea Party, The Pet *and* For Fear of the Night, *while amongst his collections are* Tales from the Nightside, A Glow of Candles *and* Nightmare Seasons. *He is the editor of the popular* Shadows, Midnight *and* Greystone Bay *series of anthologies, and his story 'The Generation Waltz' (from our Winter 1984 issue) can currently be found in our* Best Horror *book.*

THE THIEVERY OF YISH

Lin Carter

In Simrana they speak of Yish, that most misfortunate of all the thieves that dwelt in Abzoor in the land of Yeb.

The tale tells that when Yish connived to burgle the house of Pnash, his colleagues in the Stealthy Science looked dubiously at one another, with little despairing shrugs, and privately deemed him demented. But this was not so; for Yish had for too long endured the worst of luck, and in his extremity of need bethought him of Pnash, and of the many treasures of Pnash.

That Pnash was also an enchanter was a datum he dismissed as trivial and irrelevant, despite the wise adage that it is never wholesome to offend wizards.

No, poverty was his argument, and an eloquent one. As Yish put it: Why should I starve in tatters, gnawing a savourless crust, when brethren of my craft go clad in luminous silks and speak familiarly of meat?

Now, the house of Pnash stood at some remove from the city of Abzoor amidst the plains of Nuth. And it was common knowledge to the thieves of Abzoor that every approach to the residence of the enchanter was Peculiarly Guarded. Of this fact Yish took cautious note, and chose for the night of his venturings a moonless and a dark, trusting to evade discovery in the velvet glooms of midnight.

*He ransacked shelves and sacks, boxes, bales and bureaus,
but nowhere were to be found the treasures of Pnash. (Artist:
Russ Nicholson)*

Forth from the lion-guarded gates of the city he slunk, wrapped in an ebon cloak, and across the plain he glided as silently as do the shadows that the dim stars cast from the scudding clouds. And as he drew nigh unto his goal, he perceived high towers that ringed the house of Pnash about, and his heart sank into his shabby boots when he realized that these were Watchtowers. In the upper works of the nearer of these he could clearly perceive the square and stony, lidless Eye maintaining its stolid and unsleeping vigilance over the plain.

But, for a change, fortune looked favorably on Yish, for at that very moment a wild thing burst from the bushes to lope away, and the Tower turned its granite gaze to follow the thing in its flight, whereby could Yish sidle by its base and pass unseen. And under his breath, Yish thanked the little gods that, however half-heartedly, watch over those of the thievish craft.

The house of Pnash was long and low, with little evil windows like shrewd, sleepy eyes under the lowering brows of the roof. The lock on the door was large and strong; but also it was old and rusty, and Yish tried thirty of the keys on the iron ring he wore on his belt before he found the one that worked.

Within he found thick shadows, and heaps and mounds of ancient books, and piles of pots and jugs and jars, each labelled in queer Eastern characters; and everywhere were cobwebs and dust, enough to make a thief less clever than Yish betray himself with a sneeze.

He ransacked shelves and sacks, boxes, bales and bureaus, but nowhere were to be found the treasures of Pnash. Now, concerning these treasures the thieves of Abzoor were of several minds. Some said the wizard owned the nine rarest gems beknown to men, each being the only one of its kind, and each prised from a stone fallen from the Moon.

Whereas others claimed him to possess The Song of Sith, that most precious of all poems, each of whose thirty flawless lines is terminated with a rhyme for *orange*, and which is accounted the chiefest treasure of the Kings of Yeb, who kept it in a casket hewn from an single and prodigious emerald. Yet others whispered of a most marvelous Singing Flower, whose entrancing sweetness is coveted by emperors, and which was fetched by wizardry from the orchid-scented jungles of Nasht, wherein dream the forgotten ivory palaces of princes remembered only in song.

The fact was that no one knew! But, of a surety, Pnash guards his treasures jealously and with exceeding craft; hence the treasure must assuredly be one of fabulous rarity and worth.

At length Yish descended into the cellars of the house, discovering them to be gloomy and cluttered and unpleasant. He did not at all like the glass retorts filled with bubbling fluids, wherefrom the weird effulgence of clarified phosphorous glowed with cold and clammy luminance. Neither did he care for the dripping walls of ragged stone where the skeletons of children dangled piteously in rust-gnawed chains. And he little liked the tall black lectern made of gallows-wood and coffin-planks, or the huge, worm-riddled book which lay open thereupon, exhuding the unsubtle foetor of decay.

He *particularly* did not like the lectern, for the enchanter himself sat behind it, hunched on a high stool, regarding Yish with an unambiguous lack of hospitality in his yellow eyes . . .

Yish said nothing, for there was, after all, rather little that came to mind to say. And he felt quite uncomfortable in the glare of those yellow eyes. Moreover, it added nothing at all to his peace of mind—such as it was—that those eyes did not ever blink and neither did they possess the iris or the pupil commonly found in the eyes of ordinary men.

Then the enchanter smiled, and poor Yish felt even less comfortable than before: for, in lieu of teeth, the jaws of the magician were lined with rows of pointed diamonds.

"Have you come hither for the Song of Sith," he inquired pleasantly, "or for certain gems downfallen from the Moon, or was it for the Singing Flower?" The tone of his voice, though harsh, was mild, and filled with friendly curiosity.

With some effort, Yish built a smile. It was a shoddy specimen, true, but under the circumstances, we should consider it a commendable effort.

Without waiting for a reply to his query, the enchanter then stepped upon a stone and one portion of the wall sank soundlessly as a falling leaf from sight, exposing a black cavity.

"Herein you will find my treasures," said Pnash softly. "It has

taken me many lifetimes to accumulate this collection, and of
it I feel an honest pride."

He then snapped bony fingers, creating a sourceless light.
Curious despite his admittedly precarious position, Yish peered
within the opening to marvel at a row of marble statues. These
were in the likenesses of men, either lean and crafty or plump
and cunning: and all were remarkably lifelike.

"This is my collection of thieves," Pnash said with a nasty and
glittering grin. And Yish had barely time enough to commend
his spirit to those little gods that, however half-heartedly, watch
over those of the thievish craft . . . and to the tale of Yish there
is not a happy ending.

Or so, at least, they tell it in Simrana.

The last time Lin Carter *appeared in these pages was with 'The
Laughter of Han' in our Spring 1982 issue. We looked forward
to welcoming him back with the following fantastic fable, but
sadly Lin died of a heart attack in February this year, aged
only 57. In 1967 he edited and revised Robert E. Howard's* King
Kull *for book publication and this led to his long collaboration
with L. Sprague de Camp on the* Conan *series of fragments
and new stories. Lin began editing the acclaimed 'Ballantine
Adult Fantasy' line in 1969, bringing many obscure and
worthwhile books back into print, and he also edited five
volumes of* Flashing Swords, *six volumes of* The Year's Best
Fantasy Stories *and four volumes of the paperback* Weird Tales.
*His first published story was 'Masters of the Metropolis' (1956),
written with Randall Garrett, and he went on to produce a
number of heroic fantasy/adventure series featuring such
characters and settings as Thongor, Zarkon, World's End,
Callisto and the Green Star. For his efforts in the resurgence
of the fantasy field, Lin Carter will always be remembered.*

VAMPIRE VILLAGE
Guy N. Smith

"Verboten is a bad place, Sabat", the girl muttered. Sabat's expression did not change. A finger stroked the vivid scar down his left cheek as though it still throbbed, a reminder of his SAS days when he had learned to kill, silently and ruthlessly. Long dark hair accentuated his sallow complexion and his narrow deep-sunken eyes seemed almost dreamy. His jet black moustache had been recently trimmed and between his even white teeth rested a well-mellowed meerschaum pipe, smoke trickling up lazily from the bowl.

Ingrid Bacher experienced a sense of awe that partly nullified her terror. This then was Sabat, *the* Sabat. Last year the German papers had carried a story about this man, a sensational leader article. A group of fascists had sought to resurrect the Nazi regime, had tried to spread mass hysteria across the continent, a pseudo vampire army who killed their victims with a type of syringe that sucked the blood from the jugular vein. Their leader a man who claimed to be the Fuhrer reborn. But this man who sat opposite her in the small German inn was the one who had defeated them, killed as ruthlessly as they killed. There were other stories about him, too, but this was no time to dwell upon them. Suffice that he was here, had turned up as though his keen nose had scented blood again.

She stood about three yards from him, seemed to glide and then stop again, her complexion so white that he saw every detail of her features. (Artist: Andrew Smith)

"Tell me more about Verboten", he spoke softly as though to prevent the others in the room overhearing him.

"It used to be just a pretty little tourist village", she played nervously with a strand of blonde hair, pursed her lips as though she didn't really want to discuss it. "Then about five years ago a group of businessmen from Bremen came up with what they thought was a brilliant idea for making their fortunes. As you know, Transylvania has been commercialised, they have a Dracula castle and everything spooky that the tourist wants to see. Well, these men decided to bill Verboten as a vampire village. They bought everybody out, virtually rebuilt it. *Mein Gott*, they made a good job of it! None of the people from here would go anywhere near it even by day. The men created their own fake legends, at least we *thought* they were fake. Then strange things began to happen. People went missing, were glimpsed at night by passing motorists, shrouded figures skulking by the roadside. But the idea had gone too far. Suddenly people were afraid to go to Verboten, the tourist trade virtually died, and now there is nobody there. At least", she paled, "nobody *human!*"

"I see", Sabat knocked his pipe out in the ashtray, "so the spoof backfired on them?"

"You believe the story?"

"Certainly. Don't you?"

"Of course, particularly now. Oh, Sabat, isn't there anything we can do to save Gerd?"

'We may possibly be able to save his soul", Sabat answered her, "although I very much fear whether the body can be saved if our worst fears are realised. But *why* did he go to Verboten? Did he not know the dangers?"

"He was..is a realist", she was trembling slightly. "To Gerd the stories were all nonsense. The big house was advertised for sale in a property brochure in Hamburg, far enough away for prospective buyers not to know the tales. Gerd heard about it; the price was unbelievably cheap and he needed sizeable premises to start up a business venture. So, against my wishes, my brother went to Verboten to view the property. He went in the morning, last Tuesday, and promised to return before dark just to put my mind at rest. Sabat", she faltered and for a moment he thought that she was going to break down, "Gerd has not been seen or heard of since!"

Once again Mark Sabat's expression did not betray his feelings, the tightening of his stomach muscles, the tensing of every nerve in his body. The old story, one that had become a worn out hack theme for midnight horror movies. But familiarity had bred contempt, the danger was just as potent as it had always been.

"You are the one man in the whole world who could possibly help me", there was a note of pleading in her voice now. "And to think that by sheer coincidence you happened to be passing through this village, only five kilometres away from the dreaded Verboten."

"Fate plays some funny tricks", Sabat smiled, struck a match and attempted to get his pipe going again. For a few seconds Ingrid Bacher could not see his expression. "But suffice that I'm here, albeit just an ordinary tourist, but I guess we'll have to do something about your brother."

"I cannot thank you enough".

He cut short her exultation with an uplifted hand. "Don't start counting your chickens yet. The success rate is small in such matters and I'm making no promises. Tomorrow I will look into the matter. By daylight. In the meantime..."

She met his gaze, wilted beneath it. It was as though his eyes were gamma rays, melting her, goosepimpling her flesh, bringing tingling sensations to soft places. She nodded her consent.

"I live in a small house just down the street", her cherry red lips parted in a smile. "You are welcome to spend the night with me, Sabat."

Sabat drained his glass, knew that he was fully aroused. He was a stag at the rutting stand and he couldn't wait.

"Let's go", he grinned.

Sabat slept uneasily that night even though Ingrid had more than satisfied him. He felt the closeness of her body, the soft warmth of her flesh against his own naked body. She had been good, very good. Too good; and that was what worried him. She could not have been more than 18 although she had told him she was 23; there was only one place girls learned the things she had demonstrated that night—the whorehouses of Berlin. Or Paris. Not that he minded that because there were times when his own lust became too strong for him and he sought out the big city brothels. Nevertherless, he had not expected it of Ingrid.

She had quizzed him about his circumcision and he had told the truth, that an exorcist cannot risk particles of impurity secreting themselves beneath the foreskin, evil infiltrating his defences when the conflict with the powers of darkness came.

Sabat's thoughts turned to his own brother Quentin, and he smelled again the damp gravesoil from the time of their last physical encounter in that open grave in the deep woods, with the only spectators exhumed corpses. Quentin was dead, his brains blown out by Mark's revolver at point blank range. But his soul lived on—in Mark Sabat, a devilish possession, an evil that reared its head from time to time, an evil that Sabat had used on more than one occasion to fight the dark powers. And now he sensed that Quentin was stirring again, his brother's spirit alive to the presence of a new evil. Once again the malevolent powers were preparing to do battle with Sabat.

Sabat sensed the emptiness of Verboten, almost smelled the evil, a kind of living decay. Houses that had been altered by the German speculators to give a sinister appearance now did just that regardless of the facade which they had been given. Dusty broken windows, a single street with weeds sprouting out of it, doors that creaked on rusted hinges and swung to and fro in the October wind as though trying to lure an unwary stranger to enter.

He drove slowly down the street, the speedometer needle of the silver Daimler reluctantly hovering on 10 mph. Fallen leaves gusted along the gutters and rainspots hit the car's windscreen.

"It's going to rain", Ingrid felt that she had to say something.

"Looks like it", Sabat replied, "and that building up ahead looks like the big house you were telling me about."

"That's it", she shuddered. "We'd better go in and take a look."

I'll go and take a look", Sabat eased the car into the short gravelled drive. "You will stay here until I return."

She did not argue, just watched as he killed the engine and got out, let the door slam shut behind him. He was the kind of man who got his own way, in bed or anywhere else. Memories of last night came back to her and she gave a faint sigh of satisfaction.

Maybe tonight they'd do that again. Oh yes, she was sure they would. Very sure.

Sabat paused a moment to survey the house. A big rambling place, it had once probably been the country retreat of some wealthy family from the city. So dilapidated, so familiar. You saw one almost identical to this in every cheap vampire movie. The consortium had done their homework well; dusty window panes, some either cracked or broken completely. Cobwebs that might just have been real. The front door creaked just too loudly when you pushed it, a dim and dusty hallway beyond. If you were a tourist looking for a not-so-cheap thrill you would ease your way nervously inside, have fun letting your imagination run riot. If you were a psychic investigator you moved more cautiously, tried to segregate the fakes from reality. Sabat's hand strayed inside his dark blue corduroy jacket, his fingers locating the comforting bulge of a .38 revolver nestling in the holster where previously an inside pocket had been. A modification of his own, like the bullets moulded from an old silver candlestick.

Somewhere a voice whispered. He made a supreme effort to shut it out. Quentin was awake and taunting him. Shut up you bastard. Laughter that vibrated his brain like a fit of dizziness. He steadied himself, forced himself to ignore it because it would not go away.

Perhaps the new owners had not done so much work on this place as he had thought at first glance, that it had always been like this; the evil had already been here so they had left it as it was. A real bogey house for the enjoyment of visitors.

He went up the creaking woodworm-ridden stairs and began an exploration of the upper storey. Sparsely furnished, some of the furniture original, the rest bought from some junk shop that was probably delighted to get rid of its surplus rubbish in one fell swoop. Everywhere was thick with dust, the stench of decay almost overpowering. Sabat examined the floors; there were no footprints apart from his own. He had not really expected to find any.

Back downstairs, looking for a cellar entrance and finding it beneath the stairs. Quentin was still whispering; *go on down Mark, take a look in the cellar.*

Sabat flicked on his small torch, saw how the chipped and

cracked stone steps went down into a black abyss below, the walls running with condensation, the stonework green with slime. The foul odour came up at him, a smell that reminded him of putre-fying flesh. Dead rats probably. Revolver in one hand, torch in the other, he descended slowly, counting the steps as he went. Twenty-seven. It was a big cellar, probably extended to the whole area of the foundations of the house, the kind of place where wealthy families stored their wine. The kind of place where . . . .

The sight of the coffin on a raised bier came as no surprise to Sabat, more a confirmation of his own deductions. Of course there would be one. He approached it cautiously, tapped the lid sharply with the barrel of his .38. Plastic!

And there would also be a body inside. He lifted the lid; it came up easily, too easily, and he shone his torch on to the stereotyped wax features of a man clothed in flowing black garments, huge fangs protruding from the gruesome stretched mouth. He almost laughed, and for the moment Quentin was silent. The Vampire Count; probably there was some hidden device somewhere that could be worked to make him sit up, a steady raising of the cof-fin lid, a hissing sound coming out of those stretched lips, maybe even a trickle of synthetic blood.

Sabat let the lid fall back, turned away. His torch beam swept round the cellar; it wasn't as large as he had supposed, possibly at some time had been blocked off. A little shiver ran up his spine, spread up into his scalp. The family tomb next door? If so, then there was no way he was going to break through into it. He shrugged, attempted to ignore Quentin's mocking laughter and turned back towards the steps. There was evil here all right, but he had not located it; the evil would remain and there was nothing he could do about it. An exorcism might or might not work but it was none of his business.

He started momentarily as his torch picked out something hang-ing close to the ceiling, a multi-legged thing with eyes that flickered redly, swinging to and fro gently. Sabat laughed softly. A tarantula spider, the oversize rubber species which you could buy in most joke shops. God, this was a sick set-up, a con that the public revelled in, a weird mixture of fantasy with terrible reality lurking in the shadows.

He went back upstairs and outside. If Gerd was here then the ultimate evil had claimed him. *He's here, all right.* Then he's all yours Quentin.

Sabat descended the outside steps, walked back across the mossy gravelled drive. And then he stopped, felt his heart flip and his flesh began to creep again, invisible icy fingers stroking him right the way up to the nape of his neck. The Daimler was parked exactly where he had left it, a majestic silver giant reflecting the weak rays of the late October sunshine. Nothing wrong there except that . . . he stared again to make sure. *The passenger door hung open and there was no sign of Ingrid Bacher!*

Sabat tried to shout down Quentin as he battled for a logical explanation. She's got bored, gone for a look around the village. *Nobody looks around Verboten.* She's gone for a pee in the bushes. *She's gone to Gerd, Mark. You won't find her now.*

Sabat brought himself under control, became the powerful functioning machine once more, the way the SAS had trained him during those earlier years when your life depended upon alertness and clear thinking. OK, they might have got her but there was still time to find her. It was daylight, they could not have harmed her yet. He would search this place dubbed the 'Vampire Village', every house and outbuilding. And if he didn't find her . . . He smiled grimly to himself. He would face the inevitable only when he was forced to.

It was early evening by the time Mark Sabat was satisfied that he had searched the whole village. Jesus Christ, the lengths some people would go to to make money! But the ghouls who flocked here to wallow in the sick reconstruction of ancient folklore were as bad. Houses where bats hung from the ceilings on lengths of elastic, synthetic cobwebs that brushed against you, gory wax vampires, their faces twisted with indescribable agony as they writhed with stakes protruding from their chests. If this village had not been evil before, it certainly was now. The right atmosphere had been created and that was all that the forces of darkness needed. Now Verboten was *their* domain.

Sabat had not found Ingrid, and now he had to face up to the fact that he wasn't going to. He blamed himself, he should have taken her with him, kept a strict watch on her. Instead he had left her alone and defenceless. She had been lured away by some ruse, and when the sun set she would be gone forever. *His* fault. No, Quentin's! His brother's spirit had dulled his thinking, forced him into making the one mistake that *they* wanted him to make.

He considered an exorcism of the big house, dismissed the idea almost at once. It wasn't just this house, it was every one in Verboten, a mammoth task which would take him days. And there were too many of them, a concentration of evil that even he could not match. He sat there on the steps, smoked a pipe of sweet-smelling coarse stranded tobacco and knew what he had to do.

He rose to his feet, went back to the Daimler, reversed it so that its sleek nose was pointing back towards the stone pillars of the drive entrance, killed the engine again but left the ignition key in. Then he reached over into the back and found the black leather briefcase which he always carried with him, the tools of his trade which had served him on many occasions in the past. Now he needed them more than he had ever needed them in his life before.

Finally, just as the deep red sun was beginning to dip behind the wooded hills to the west, he went back inside the big house.

It was nearly time.

Dusk had the shadows moving out from the recesses of the big hallway where they had lurked during the daylight hours, patches of blackness that crept across the damp stone floor as though they were reaching out to claim this human who had dared to linger in Verboten.

Sabat eased the .38 in his holster, had confidence enough in his own fast draw, speed enough to beat an adversary unless it crept up on him from behind. He made sure that his back was against the stone wall. Watching and waiting, those shadows growing longer, reaching out for him. Quentin was strangely silent as though he, too, was waiting.

Sabat's thoughts were grasshopping, remembering those years in priesthood when he first recognised his talent for exorcism. His disillusionment, the SAS; he would probably have still been with them had it not been for a certain Colonel's wife who had an obsession with whips and canes and a streak of sadism which transcended his own. Catriona Lealan; Ingrid Bacher reminded him of her in a different sort of way. Her lust, her . . .

And then he saw her, but this time Ingrid Bacher was not in his imagination. She stood about three yards from him, seemed to glide and then stop again, her complexion so white that he saw every detail of her features. Beautiful, but spoiled when her lips parted in a smile that was more of a vulpine snarl, those perfect white teeth suddenly much larger. The full red lips slobbered and the eyes seemed to glow redly. Watching him, a snarling she-wolf about to spring.

"I'm afraid I haven't found Gerd", Sabat's voice was even, they might have been conducting a casual conversation again in that inn a few miles back down the road.

"You won't", her head went back and she laughed shrilly. "You won't find him, Sabat, *because he doesn't exist*! The only brothers and sisters I have are in this place, waiting for *you* tonight!"

"I see", he smiled mirthlessly and rose to his feet. "You are the lure, the bait to trap Sabat. But I'd be interested to know why you place such great importance on my presence here. You weren't one of them last night, I know that for certain."

"Correct", her eyes narrowed. "But they took my parents, my friends, one by one over the past months. They left me for a purpose." She moved a pace closer, lowered her voice almost as though she was afraid of being overheard. "They knew you were not far away, Sabat, that you might come hunting us as you hunted and destroyed others. Madeleine Gaufridi, Louis Nevillon, Petraux, the French sorcerer who like yourself had two souls. Oh yes, Sabat, you have a lot to answer for. They spared me so that I could bring you here where they may take their revenge."

"And your reward?" Sabat's eyes never left her.

"They will give my parents and myself eternal peace."

"You fool!" Sabat laughed harshly. "You poor innocent fool. They will not set you free. You are condemned to be one of the living dead for eternity."

Ingrid recoiled as though she had been struck by a physical blow, those eyes reflecting a fear deep within her, a moment of doubt. Then her expression changed again, one of sheer malevolence, a burning hatred inside the shape which had once been a living body. She thrust her head forward, hissed through those sharp grotesque teeth.

"Remember last night, Sabat? That will be *our* reward, the two of us together for eternity."

"No", his features hardened and as he spoke he raised his right hand, held aloft a small silver crucifix which seemed to glow with an ethereal light in the deepening dusk. "In the name of the Father, and the Son and . . ."

Ingrid Bacher screamed, a terrible sound that came from the depths of a soul which was no longer her own, staggered backwards. "No, Sabat. *No!*"

And that was when Sabat shot her. The report of the .38 thundered in the empty hallway, the orange stab of flame briefly driving those dark shadows back into their corners. The silver bullet took Ingrid in the centre of her forehead, split the skull, showering splinters of bone. But no blood flowed as she sank slowly down to the floor. Of all the creatures of the night in this place Sabat knew that she at least was at peace.

He moved fast, felt them coming for him even as he ran for the partly open door. Whispered cries of rage that could have come from Quentin, shapes in the darkness that kept their distance only because of the crucifix which he, Sabat, held out before him. "In the name of the Father, and the Son, and the Holy Ghost. Yea, though I walk in the valley of the shadow of death, I will fear no evil." It was keeping them at bay but for how long? They were strong, very strong, and they wanted him badly.

Outside the wind had risen to gale force, was tearing at his clothing, trying to drive him back inside. Icy fingers clawed at him but somehow he made it as far as the Daimler, flung himself into the driving seat, slammed the door shut, but he knew that that would not keep *them* out. Faces against the window, things that had no right to exist, that no human being should be forced to look upon. And Quentin was laughing shrilly.

Sabat's one fear was that the engine might not fire but it did not fail him. A low purr, rising to a crescendo as he got his revs, shot forward, the powerful headlights showing a host of deathly white shapes trying to bar his way. He drove at them, braced himself for the impact but there was none. The stone pillars loomed up and he shot between them, out into the road, the main street of a dead village that had suddenly come to life.

Hands clawed for the Daimler as it gathered speed, hideous faces screwed up into dead masks of fur spat and screamed at

Sabat as he accelerated. They were running, gliding after him, shrill voices penetrating his brain and drowning even Quentin's screams of frustration. A young child darted into Sabat's path and he almost braked. And then she was gone, back into the darkness where she would live for eternity, a tormented soul claimed by the dark ones.

Suddenly he was clear of the village. The trees no longer bent double, the wind had dropped, and a half moon cast its silvery glow across the surrounding countryside. Sabat eased back in his seat, tried to relax. The souls of those he had destroyed in life had tried to lure him to Verboten for their final act of revenge, a plan that had so very nearly succeeded. Ingrid Bacher, their final pawn, had failed them when with her guile she could surely have tempted Sabat for one last time. But that night of love had still lingered inside her, even after they had taken her, and she had hesitated.

And Sabat had repaid her for her love with eternal peace.

Guy N. Smith's *first published novel—now long out of print— was* Werewolf by Moonlight *in 1973, but he became much more widely known with a string of popular horror novels that had more punchy titles:* Killer Crabs, Night of the Crabs, The Sucking Pit, The Slime Beast, Mania *and* Fiend, *to give a few examples. Grafton Books will be reissuing some of the above titles next year. Guy has also published several film novelizations, including* The Sleeping Beauty *and* Snow White! *For the past few years New English Library has been issuing a series of novels under the collective title 'Sabat'. The four volumes published to date are* The Graveyard Vultures, The Blood Merchants, Cannibal Cult *and* The Druid Connection. *Mark Sabat, an ex-priest, SAS-trained killer and exorcist has a mission to hunt down and destory his mortal enemy, his brother, who has chosen the Left Hand Path of Evil. This is the first Sabat short story.*

It took a few seconds to realize that the old man had been staring at her. (Artist: Alan Hunter)

THE FARMER AND THE TRAVELLING SALESMAN'S DAUGHTER

C. Bruce Hunter

It was the summer after Sandy Pierce finished the ninth grade at Jefferson Davis Junior High. A few months earlier she had successfully negotiated algebra, English and general science and had learned and quickly forgotten a substantial amount of history. Now she curled up restlessly in the passenger seat of her father's old "woody" station wagon, while dreams of the school's halls and lockers and lunchrom caressed her lightly sleeping mind. The rumble of the car's balding tires on the gravel had lulled her to sleep in spite of her cramped position. And it was only the car's swaying as it rounded curves that kept bringing her back into the harsh world of Georgia's summer heat.

After a long day of baking the earth, the sun was almost down. Still, it came through the windshield so low that the visors could not shut it out, and its yellow glare added to the sweltering air that seemed to hang motionless, in spite of the ventialtion coming through the woody's open windows.

"Daddy?" Sandy mumbled, dreamily opening her eyes.

Tom Pierce paid no attention. He just kept driving, looking alternately through the windshield and out the side windows as if he expected to see a band of customers come riding over the nearest hill to meet his wagon and trade for the thread and toiletries and gaudy costume jewelry he carried in suitcases now only loosely filled after three days of traveling the back roads.

Sandy shifted her position, wincing slightly when the numbness in her legs changed to a painful tingling. Her close cropped hair felt wet at the back and sides as her head rolled against the seat back.

"Daddy, when will we stop?" she pleaded.

"Soon, honey," he answered, though perhaps it wasn't really an answer. It might just as well have been an absent-minded reflex.

Cresting a low hill, the car started a gentle descent into a wide basin that stretched out through occasional stands of pines and a scraggly patchwork of tall grass and red clay.

Sandy mumbled something else, but her father continued scanning the horizon for several seconds more before reacting.

"All right, honey," he finally said. "We'll look for a place to spend the night."

They drove another three or four miles without seeing anything promising. Then, as the car rattled around another curve, they noticed something off to the left. There, set well away from the road on the other side of a field of peanuts whose green bushes rippled gently in the evening breeze, stood a small white farmhouse flanked by weathered grey outbuildings.

"Can we stop here, Daddy?" Sandy asked. She had given up on trying to sleep and was now sitting upright as close to the window as she could manage.

"I guess so," Tom said. "It's probably too late to do any more selling today, anyway."

He located an unpaved drive that skirted the peanut field and turned the station wagon onto its deep-rutted surface. The car bounced and shimmied up to the house, and there it sighed when he turned off its engine and let it coast to a stop.

While Sandy stretched, he got out and walked toward the house. He climbed a pair of cinder block steps and crossed the porch's sagging floor boards, but before he could knock the door opened to reveal a man in faded overalls and a stained T-shirt.

Tom instinctively feigned his professional smile and extended his hand.

"Pardon me, sir," he said. "My name is Tom Pierce. I'm a salesman and . . ." The door started to close in his face. " . . . my daughter and I are looking for a place to spend the night."

The door opened again and the farmer reappeared. A faint smile formed on his grey-bristled face as he looked beyond Pierce to the car, where Sandy had gotten out and was limping around to get the circulation back into her legs.

Hinges creaked as the door opened wider and the farmer leaned against the jamb.

"I reckon I can make room for you," he said, rubbing the stubble on his chin with the tips of his forefinger and thumb. "Is they just the two of you?"

"Yes, just me and my daughter, Sandy. We've been on the road all day and . . ."

"Well," the farmer interrupted, "she can stay in my daughter's room, and I guess you can bunk in with me."

"Are you sure we won't be putting your daughter out?" Tom said, stepping quickly forward to accept the invitation before it could be withdrawn.

"She ain't here," the farmer said.

He retreated into the house with a beckoning gesture. Tom went in and Sandy, whose limp had eased to a slightly uneven stride, ran to catch up. She bounded up the steps, across the porch and followed her father into the living room, where she encountered the mixed smells of frying pork chops and cornbread.

The farmer was already in the kitchen fumbling with a jumble of plates in the drying rack beside the sink.

"You're welcome to some food if you're hungry," he called over his shoulder. "I just butchered a hog and there's plenty of fresh pork."

"Thanks." Tom followed him into the kitchen. "We haven't had supper yet, and some home cooking would go really good right now."

Sandy lagged behind in the living room to survey a sight she had never seen before. It was so unlike the suburban houses she was accustomed to. Instead of beige wallpaper and brocade drapes, the room had four plain walls of light blue smudged in places with grey-brown dirt. Where the hall mirror and shelves

of bric-a-brac should have been, there were a feed store calen-
dar, a large picture of Jesus and an assortment of family photos
taped directly to the wall. It was a new world, and somehow she
found its rustic bluntness fascinating.

She took in as much of it as possible before drifting into the
kitchen, where plates of meat and vegetables and a pan of cornbread were already laid out on an unpainted hardwood table. She
sat in the chair that was offered to her and started eating
mechanically while she examined, one by one, a menagerie of
strange and wonderful utensils that looked as if they belonged
more in a museum than in a tiny house so far from town.

She soon started to feel uncomfortable, though. It took a few
seconds for her to realize that the old man had been staring at
her while she was, perhaps rudely, examining his house. She
blushed and lowered her head self-consciously.

"Oh, don't mind me looking at you," he said when he saw that
he had embarrassed her. "It's just that you favour my daughter
Nancy a lot. Especially your hair. It's the colour of yeller gold,
just like my Nancy's."

Sandy smiled and touched the side of her head. She felt as if
she had just been welcomed into this exciting little world. And
she knew that for the rest of the night she would feel very much
at home.

There was little talk during the meal. All three of them were
tired and hungry. They passed the plates of food around the table
and ate quietly while the sun eased behind the horizon.

After supper, while Tom Pierce sat alone in the living room
adding up his invoices and receipts, Sandy helped with the dishes.
It seemed the thing to do.

The farmer washed and she dried. She moved slowly, like a
child trying to make a game last as long as possible. And all the
time she enjoyed looking at the old man and his kitchen full of
marvelous treasures. When they had finally done all there was
to do, she put the last of the knives and forks into the rack and
wiped her hands with the dish rag she had used to dry them.

The farmer ambled into the living room, stretching and flex-
ing his legs to ease the stiffness in them.

"I've got to get up early in the morning," he said to Sandy or
to her father; it wasn't clear which. "I guess I'll be going to bed,

but you all can stay up if you want."

Tom closed his invoice book and laboriously pulled himself from his chair. "We might as well turn in, too," he yawned. "It's been a long day, and we've got a long way to go tomorrow."

Sandy nodded gratefully and draped the dish rag over the drying rack. Stifling a yawn, she rubbed her eyes and wandered back into the living room.

The farmer disappeared into the hallway at the back of the house to turn on a light there, then he came back to turn off the ones in the kitchen and living room. Finally, he led his guests down the hall to a pair of doors that stood across from each other.

"This here is Nancy's room." He showed Sandy the room on the right. "Just make yourself at home." Then he stood aside to let her go in.

Sandy entered the room. The table lamp was already on, and the room was bright and clean, though slightly musty from disuse. The bed was made, and the closet door stood open to reveal a line of neatly hung clothes waiting for their owner's return.

The room was not unlike her own, Sandy thought. She could be comfortable here. She smiled tired approval and turned to close the door before getting undressed.

As the light in the hallway dimmed to a narrow wedge, the farmer led Tom into the other room, stabbing at the wall switch with one finger as he went in. This room was plain. There were only a double bed, its sheets in disarray, a straight backed chair and an old, age-darkened dresser. Standing close beside the bed, the dresser held a Bible with a pair of glasses resting on it, a lamp and a water glass and a bottle of prescription medicine. Along one wall ran a row of shoulder-high nails, each supporting two or three coat hangers. A few of them were empty, but most held a shirt or coat or pair of trousers.

"You care which side of the bed you have?" the farmer asked, but he was already walking around to what was obviously his side.

"It doesn't matter," Tom answered. "I'll probably be asleep too soon for it to make any difference."

They started taking their clothes off. Tom removed his necktie without undoing the knot and looped it over the back of the chair. His shirt went on top of the tie and his trousers, neatly folded, in the seat and his shoes, a sock stuffed in each, under the chair.

The farmer was now in his underwear, too. He had draped his clothes over the dresser and slipped his shoes under the bed. He tossed one of the two pillows across the bed for his guest to use and propped the other one up against the headboard on his side.

"If you don't care, I'll do some reading before going to sleep," he said. Without waiting for an answer, he sat down on the bed, pulled his legs up and leaned back into the pillow.

"You won't bother me at all," Tom said as he slid between the sheets. The well used mattress gave easily under his weight. He squirmed a little to find a comfortable position while the farmer put on his glasses, took the Bible from the dresser and opened it to the pages marked by its yellow ribbon. The farmer moved his lips slightly as he started reading.

Tom rolled over onto his side, turning his back to the lamp's glare, and nestled his head deeper into the pillow. He closed his eyes and it was not long before he floated into oblivion.

The next thing he knew the room was filled with a different light and a bird was chirping nonstop in the branches of a tree just outside the window. At the sound of a squirrel thumping across the roof, he sat up and looked around the room.

The other side of the bed was empty. The place his host had occupied was now marked only by a depression in the mattress and a pattern of rumples and creases that spread across the sheet. The Bible was on the dresser, open and face down, and the door was closed.

Tom stretched and started to get out of bed. The morning heat was just beginning to come through the open window, and he had to pull himself free of sheets still wet from a summer night's perspiration. But the floor was pleasantly cool, and he walked around the room as he got dressed to take advantage of the feeling. He reversed the previous night's ritual, taking his clothes from the chair one piece at a time and checking each to be sure that it was not too wrinkled to wear through another day of door to door selling.

At the end of the ritual, he buttoned his shirt, tucked it into his trousers and slipped on his necktie as he walked across the room and opened the door that led into the hall.

At one end of the hall, a back door stood open. Two flies flitted on the inside of the screen trying to find a rusted out hole through which they might escape, and on the outside a wasp batted against the screen trying to get in.

The other bedroom door was still closed. Tom was about to wake Sandy, but just as he was raising his fist to knock, he paused.

The sweet smell of cooking breakfast suddenly came to him from the other end of the hall. He inhaled deeply and decided to let his daughter sleep a little longer. The trip had been hard on her; she was not accustomed to traveling the back roads, and she could probably use an extra half hour of sleep.

He turned away from her door and walked down the hall and into the kitchen. There, the farmer was standing at the stove, holding an old iron skillet by the handle and pushing its contents around with a fork. When he noticed Tom, he looked up and smiled.

"Come on in," he said, pointing to a chair at the table. "Did you sleep well?"

"Yes, I slept like the dead," Tom said. "I didn't move until a few minutes ago. How about you?"

"Oh, I been up for a couple of hours. Been out to the smoke house putting up some sausage and salting hams."

Tom slid into the chair. On the table an empty plate and coffee cup awaited him. On one side of the plate, a stack of toast filled a saucer, and across from that a jelly glass half full of sugar was flanked by salt and pepper shakers.

The farmer took a pot of coffee from the stove and brought it over to pour some of the jet black liquor into Tom's cup, then he returned to the stove while Tom spooned sugar into the coffee and stirred it.

"You never did say where your daughter is," he said as he lifted the cup and tested the steaming coffee with his lips.

"She's gone." The farmer carried the frying pan to the table and forked two patties of sausage onto the plate.

Tom quickly pried one of them apart with his spoon and popped it into his mouth. He chewed the hot meat gingerly and washed it down with a gulp of coffee. As soon as he had swallowed it, he took another bite and this time cut its strong, peppery taste with a piece of toast from the saucer.

"A salesman like you come through here last summer," the farmer said as he returned the frying pan to the stove. "He asked to stay, and I took him in and gave him food and a place, just like the Good Book says to do. And you know how he repaid me?"

Tom shook his head and stuffed more food into his mouth.

"He fooled with my daughter Nancy. That's how. Then he went on about his business and left her to pay for it."

"I'm sorry to hear that," Tom said between sips of coffee.

"Made her pregnant, he did," the farmer continued. "She carried his bastard for a few months, but she couldn't bear the shame of it, and all the people hereabouts knowing what she done. So she finally up and killed herself."

Tom stopped chewing. His words were muffled through a mouthful of sausage and bread.

"I hope you don't blame all salesmen for what that one did."

At first the farmer didn't answer. He turned his back and reached into a drawer to pull out a whetstone. After a long pause he finally said, "Eat up, young feller."

Tom turned again to his plate and started to cut off another piece of sausage. Then he stopped. He reached down with a finger and thumb and teased a short, blond hair from the half eaten patty. He started gagging as he pushed his chair from the table.

Meanwhile at the stove, the farmer gently—almost lovingly— stroked the blade of a butcher knife back and forth across the whetstone.

C. Bruce Hunter is a lexicographer and writer of fantasy and mystery stories whose work has appeared in such diverse publications as Alfred Hitchcock's Mystery Magazine, Woman's World *and, of course,* Fantasy Tales. *He is the co-editor of the* New Webster's Computer Dictionary, *but his previous employment has included work as a travelling salesman in North Carolina, where he lives. Some of his real-life experiences from this job led him to pen a trilogy of stories, of which the following is the second.* The Travelling Salesman and the Farmer's Daughter *appeared in our tenth anniversary issue and* The Salesman and the Travelling Farmer's Daughter *is forthcoming. Each of the stories stands on its own, and although the author tells us he has actually met the characters he describes, the present offering is predominantly fiction!*

FANCY THAT

J.N. Williamson

"**F**ancy meeting you here!" A pleased resonance.

"Well, I like *that*! Who else would you expect to meet in your bedroom, mister?"

"It certainly isn't like the old days." Mock sigh. "Hold on, don't turn away. Please. I was only joking."

Mood shift. "I'm so glad you married me this morning." Genuine pause of concern. "It *was* this morning. Wasn't it?"

"—Was it? Feels like an eternity. Wait; that isn't a joke, honey. It really does seem like some while ago. Or, always. I'm confused about it."

"Darling, it doesn't matter when we got married. Only that we were. And are."

"Look, beautiful, let's meet this way every now and then. All right?"

A smile to be recognized, experienced, by others senses. "I'm not sure we even have a choice about it. But this is special; I *want* to be with you, this way . . . 'Night."

"Night."

"**F**ancy meeting you this way." The hint of a chuckle.

"I'm not here now because I wished to be! I know about *her*, and what you did."

"But I didn't . . . All right, you've got me. I can't lie, *this* way." With great earnestness, and again now: "But I only kissed her once or twice. Well—three or four times. That's all."

"At a time when I scarcely even felt like a woman!"

"That's why I—the *other* part of 'me'—did it." Anguished sigh. "Because, being pregnant, you don't feel pretty, don't feel like you. When you're *you*, you're always pretty to me. Always."

"Perhaps that's the truth. I don't think we can lie, this way. But don't do it again, darling. Please? We have made us as we're meant to be—but either of us can change that, can spoil it forever. I sense that—don't you?"

"I do. And I'm sorry." Awkward, tender pause. "Wish I could touch you now. Put my arm around you."

"Remember, tomorrow, that you want to." Urgency, stridently but sweetly. "And try not to let your pride get in the way."

"I will. And try not to forget that I love *all* of you, *all* you *are*. 'Night."

" 'Night."

Fancy meeting you after all this . . . *whatever* it is."

"Darling, we must talk. This way." Concerned hum of need.

"You absolutely mustn't worry that, well, you *couldn't*. Last night, before sleep. You had a rough day. It wasn't your fault. You worry so much about Billy and that crowd of friends he runs with. They—"

"It isn't just that." Something quite like a sigh. "I'm not forty yet, but I'm—I'm over the hill."

"Not really. Just the *other* 'you'; just temporarily!" Merriment, reassuringly.

"Honey, that other part can be important, too. Look, I can't help how I feel."

Softly, seductively. "That's why I wanted us to meet *this* way once more."

"Come *on*." Rueful, unpleasant vibrations. "What can we do this way?"

Still more softly: "Everything else, I think. Reach each other more deeply than the other way. Try. *Try*, just remembering that you love . . . all I *am*."

Out-reaching, outpouring of private, unspoken emotions.

"And try not to forget that I love all of you, all you are." (Artist: Allen Koszowski)

Openness, and receiving. Contacting, mutually experienced; known; accepted. "I do love you, babe. Oh, I *do*."

"Wasn't that lovely?" Bubbling contentment. "Hm-m, you're something special!"

"But y'didn't say 'I love you, too.' *Do* you, still, after the years—after what a fool I am—after how many times I forget *this* us?"

"Always and always, I love you. —Better?"

"*So* much. 'Night."

"Night . . ."

"Fancy my wanting to meet you here. This way. You know why, don't you?"

Distance. No fast reply. A dark, small resistance, lies impossible. "You probably desire to bully me, about our son. —No; that's not it. You never bullied anyone. But—"

"Honey, Bill has a life of his own. What's happening to him is not your fault. Or mine."

"But he's so unhappy, so miserable. He's ruining *everything*."

"No. Not everything." Very firm. "Not—us. Unless you allow it to happen."

"You've never understood for an instant what it is to be a mother, to give birth, raise them, go *on* caring—"

"But Bill's path is *his*." Even more firmly, but gently. "Now he must find himself, and someone for him. On his own. There is nothing that you and I—or *we*, when we're that by day—can do to help him find himself, and her."

"I yearn to save him, darling, so badly. He's meant so *much*. I want him to—"

"To satisfy your hopes for him; mine; ours?" Noiseless, wry laughing vibration. "I wanted this, too, remember? Remember how I tried first to get him into Olympics-style sports—then when he grew up, I wanted him to become a—"

"You were so *silly* about Billy!" The return, mercifully, of laughter. "Yet tried, showed him you cared; you were there. After awhile, darling, that was all there was for you to do."

"Which is what I have been telling *you*! One more point: As long as we both want it to be that way, more than anything else, there will always be *us*. We cannot keep Bill part of us; he never truly was. But you have me, honey, and I have you—for ever."

Sweet, snuggling sounds. "I love you. 'Night."

"Fancy this: I'm old. Not getting old. *Old*."

"Well, I like *that*! What would I want with an old person in my bedroom, Mister!"

"Beats me. You haven't gotten old at all, beautiful."

Scornful but pleased amusement. "You look at me first, always, with your daylight eyes, my love. And sometimes I think you have never seen me clearly, at all."

"Oh, yes; I have." A shaky, wandering whisper. "Those times I've had to be away from you. And *these* times, when—when I can't quite see you at all. Yet I know you best, now."

"You see me precisely as I see you, these times." A pause. "As all the things we truly are, used to be, nearly became, and *will* be, for good." Low-pitched, laugh-like vibration. "Honestly, hon, don't you understand yet what we are doing, now, and exactly what we are?"

No quick answer. "Sometimes I believe we are one another's dreams. At other moments, I think we are—ghosts, somehow. Because we meet this way only in the dark, at midnight and beyond. Yet I awaken and there's daylight and I believe you arise, too. Or is *that* the dream?"

"No, no. But this—these precious moments—are the threshold of the *long* reality, the *important*, *enduring* reality."

Irascible masculine resonance: "I don't get it! I've tried, but I do *not* understand—*this*. All I know is that you are truly you and I am I. Not as we are by day, but . . . *more*, in an odd way. And another thing I know, beautiful: That when I awaken, I never consciously remember these nocturnal meetings."

"And yet, they influence you, and me, during the period of light." A contemplative moment, as if used to gather difficult thought. "You married me in the morning of my grownup life, and I'm still glad. But of course, you don't 'consciously' remember these times, silly. These are the moments when, in our sleep, our *unconscious selves* may talk, commune—always with honesty, forever to reaffirm our love and enable us to make the waking *us* go on."

"We're our *own* ghosts, then?" Wonder; understanding. "But

how could you figure it out, how can you know?"

"Unlike you, a part of me has always remembered the night. And"—a loving, cautious pause—"the daylight time is drawing to a close."

"Should I fear it?" Wind, whispering softly across the sleeping, the aged forms, bony and brittle under the press of winter blankets. "Should I—fear—that real night that is coming?"

"Silly!" Two syllables like lips kissing. "Remember, you said that you loved '*all* of me there is?' Well, *that* is what lies ahead for you; and you are what lies ahead for me. Truly so, and for the first time: The *all* of love."

Hesitation. "I'm so tired." The slightest tremor. "'Night."

"'Night."

"**F**ancy meeting you—*here!*"

"Well, I like that! Who else would you expect to meet for eternity?"

"You're . . . lovely. And *this*—*this* is something special." Wonder; joy. "I see you, everything, *clearly* now! Good morning!"

"It is, isn't it?" Smiling satisfaction, an embrace, a loving kiss. "A very *good* morning . . . !"

One of the most prolific writers working in the horror genre, J.N. Williamson will publish his thirty-first novel early next year, called The Black School, *from Dell Books. His other novels include* The Evil One *(Zebra Books),* Noonspell *(Leisure Books) and* The Banished *(Playboy Press). He is currently writing a non-fiction work on the casebooks of ghost-hunters Ed and Lorraine Warren and by the time you read these words, Berkley Books will have published* The Best of Masques, *an anthology of stories taken from the two* Masques *anthologies he edited for Maclay publishers. A third volume,* Masques III, *will appear next year from St. Martins Press. He has published a number of short stories, such as 'The Night Seasons', which was a runner-up for last year's World Fantasy Award. Other tales are due in various anthologies this year, including* The Year's Best Fantasy Fiction.

TOUCHING

Chris Morgan

Glamorous in her see-through nightdress, Cheryl lay in bed, dreaming. She always knew when she was dreaming, and was able to influence the course of the dream—though sometimes only a little. Once she had thought herself unique in this ability, but an article in *Reader's Digest* had taught her that it was merely uncommon.

Edward had always pooh-poohed this talent of hers, confident in his opinion of her innate inferiority, while Don had listened to her description of it and then stroked her cheek in puzzled awe, but neither had ever suggested that she shouldn't exercise it.

So, sleeping soundly in the encircling arms of her second husband, Cheryl constructed dreams involving her first.

Edward stands looking out to sea. Plump with slightly receding hair cut very short and very punctiliously dressed in an out-of-fashion suit, he looks like a businessman of forty-eight. Ever since he was twenty-five he has looked like a businessman of forty-eight. In fact he is thirty-three, to Cheryl's thirty-one, and is waiting for a lady-friend. If Edward thinks of Cheryl at all at times like this he pities her for her plainness and despises her for her mouselike demeanour. He has left his three-litre Jaguar on the road above him and walked a few yards down the spongy turf to look at the waves, the rocks and the sunset. He knows that Elise, or Susan, or Hazel—Cheryl cannot decide which of them he should be expecting—will drive along the coast road, park beside his car and walk down to him. But Edward, infuriating, predictable Edward, will not look round until he hears a soft footfall on the grass behind him. Then he'll say, in an affected drawl, "We-el, hello . . ." Now he is lighting a cigarette (with the theatrical gesture which he practises whether or not he is being watched) while simultaneously stealing a glance at his gold-plated Rolex. He hears a car approaching and tenses up. It halts and, after a brief pause, its door slams. He smiles at the sunset. What he doesn't hear is the sound of the Jaguar's door being opened. He never sees the heavily muscled arm that reaches inside or the hand (the hand!) that releases the brake. The car rolls forward noiselessly but something alerts Edward. He swings round and begins to drawl, "We-el—" just as the front bumper hits his shins, scooping him into the air. Man and car go over that Dorset cliff as one.

It wasn't like that, thought Cheryl in her sleep, because it wasn't Don's style, but perhaps it should have been. Edward often met women at deserted coastal locations. He thought she didn't know about it, thought she hadn't the nerve to take a lover for herself but would stay passively and uncomplainingly at home, waiting for him. Little had he known. She hadn't just waited—she had found Don. Cheryl tried to cover Don's large hands with her own smaller, paler ones, happily clutching them to her as she drifted into deeper, non-dreaming sleep.

Cheryl knew some women who, when choosing or judging a man, looked first at the face, others at the body, particularly the bottom. For some it was the clothes and for a few the wallet. But for her it was always the hands. She couldn't abide dirty hands or scabby knuckles or bitten nails. Nor did she approve of calluses or scars. The hands were a window to the personality, though not, she had to admit, an infallible one. Edward's hands had always been clean and neat and his whole appearance was, likewise, clean and neat, but that hadn't prevented him from being a right bastard at times.

His hands had attracted her from the first. They were very white and even, with slender fingers and long nails. Long on the finger,

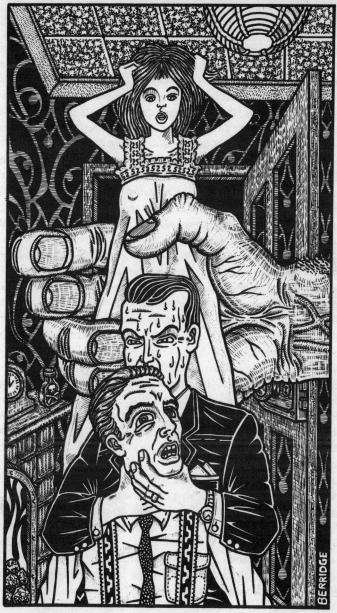

Don's beautiful, virile hands fasten themselves around Edward's neck, with strong thumbs pressing in on either side of the windpipe. (Artist: Steve Berridge)

of course, not beyond it. He had always filed his nails at least twice a week, maintaining an even white arc, just a sixteenth of an inch wide, at the end of each one. Not damaging his hands had been almost an obsession with him, so that he had worn gloves in cold weather, for driving, and when doing odd jobs around the house or garden. That his hands were almost hairless with slightly plump backs was disguised by the liberal application of gold accessories. Wristwatch, cuff links, name bracelet, signet ring and—after their marriage—a wedding ring of the same pattern as hers, all dazzled the eye and spoke—shouted, even— of his well—groomed affluence. Perhaps it was the gold that had impressed her first, not by its value but by the air of maturity and savoir faire that it lent him.

It wasn't just the *look* of his hands. They had always excited her, turned her on, especially when he stroked her neck or held her shoulders as they made love. Always, that is, until the summer they'd gone to the Cote d'Azur and she'd caught Edward amid the sand-dunes with a bronzed and brazen mademoiselle, holding *her* shoulders in just the same way. After that she'd found his hands less attractive.

Don she had met at the local squash club. Edward had always disapproved of violent exercise and tried to discourage her from going, but she ignored him and, teaming up with Susie from the next-door-but-one house, she played for an hour every Monday afternoon. It was Susie who knew Don, just slightly, and introduced them—he was there on his afternoon off, of course. Cheryl always shook hands: with Don she didn't believe it. Nobody's hand could be so perfect and at the same time so transparent a guide, yet his was. At the first touch she *knew* him: neat but pleasantly easy-going; strong but gentle; experienced yet still naive; a man who worked with hand and brain; almost certainly single; somebody she could dominate. Only then did she look at the rest of him, and was pleasantly surprised by his height, good looks and youthfulness.

Don's hands were the most ruggedly beautiful she had ever seen on a man, being large and slim, combining power with dexterity. Every vein and sinew stood out clearly, despite the sprinkling of dark hair, and the skin and nails were clean, unblemished and exquisitely well cared for. They were a pianist's hands, but Don was no pianist.

As they sat down for a cup of coffee after their respective games, Don's hand touched her bare forearm quite casually and naturally. Cheryl nearly came. She felt her face flush and her nipples stand up. Before she finished her coffee she knew not only that she had to have Don but that they would need Edward's money to live comfortably.

So Edward would have to die, and Don would have to be persuaded to kill him.

While preparing Edward's evening meal just as he liked it ("three courses, at least two of them hot, with no foreign muck and no rabbit food"), Cheryl contemplated poison. There were many possibilities, she thought, but most if not all had strings attached. The daily addition of a solution of arsenic to his food would take too long to accomplish anything—perhaps nine months to cause nothing worse than dyspepsia and a skin rash. And how could Don be on hand every day to administer the dose? Certainly she could not do it. An image came to her mind of Don hiding perpetually in her broom cupboard and coming out shortly before seven each evening to pour a dose of arsenic onto Edward's dinner. She thought of a small brown glass bottle held in those beautiful, strong hands; she watched as they uncorked it and poured. It was a lovely sight to imagine those hands doing anything whatsoever, but the idea was silly.

Something quicker-acting, perhaps? She knew that pain-killing tablets such as asprin and paracetemol were lethal poisons if one swallowed enough at a time. Yet if Don ground up, say, fifty tablets, would it be possible to mix such a heap of powder into Edward's meal so that he didn't notice it? And even if it worked, she'd heard that it took the victims several agonizing days to die from kidney failure, which wouldn't do. It was not that she wished to protect Edward from a painful death, just that if death came so slowly he would have time to speak to doctors and police, time to convince them all that his wasn't a case of suicide but of murder.

Quicker-acting still was strychnine. Her mental picture this time was of Don's wonderful hands pouring a small quantity of it onto the top of the sugar bowl. At a quick glance the granules were identical. Edward would sugar his coffee as usual—he didn't trust her to put in the requisite one and a half spoonsful—and drink it down without tasting anything strange. Then, within five or ten minutes, he would be hit by hideous muscular spasms, with limbs locking and lips curling back in a rictus of agony. (She *knew*, she had read it in detective novels.) Death would follow within another ten minutes; no chance to denounce them to the authorities. Of course, there remained the major problems of proving that Edward was the sort of person to commit suicide, and of getting the strychnine. Perhaps, after all, poisoning was not the proper modus operandi.

Cheryl bent over the sink and began to scrape some carrots.

"It'll be much better if he disappears completely," said Cheryl as she sat on the sofa beside Don. "You must kill him and then get rid of the body. I don't really mind how you kill him so long as you do it with your hands. It must be with those hands."

"But why me?" said Don.

"Because you are best fitted for the task, my dear. You are physically and mentally strong, with a very stable personality. I couldn't kill Edward because of my emotional attachment to him. After all, I am his wife, and my sensibilities wouldn't allow me to do such a thing. Also, I haven't the strength. You do understand my position, don't you? Now, come closer and stroke me again."

"Ohh, Cheryl. I still don't see why you can't divorce him."

"We need his money. Surely, my dear, you don't want to see me come down in the world and have to move out of this house into a small semi on the wrong side of town? We could barely manage to run both cars on your wages, remember. Now, do come and stroke me."

She pulled open the top of her wrap, to expose her breasts. Don reached over and laid his hands on them. Gently he caressed a nipple. She came quickly and noisily.

When she finished gasping she covered herself and said, "I think you should use a knife to do it. One deep thrust into the chest ought to kill him. Or perhaps you could cut his throat. That would splash a lot of blood around, though, so you'd need to do it over the bath. I'll invite you round for coffee one evening. You go to the bathroom, then start banging on the door pretending you can't get out. Edward will come running and you can— No! Even better, I'll tell him you're the plumber and you can carry a tool-bag containing a long, sharp knife. Then, when you're both in the bathroom—"

"Oh, shit, Cheryl. You're enjoying it! You're enjoying the thought of me stabbing Edward."

"Not at all," she said. "I'm enjoying the thought of you holding a sharp knife in your wonderful hands. It always suits you. Now, touch me again."

More than a year after the event, Cheryl was once more indulging in conscious dreaming about Edward's death.

Don and Edward stand toe to toe in the centre of the lounge. Both still hold glasses of sherry in their hands, but the last dregs of conviviality are draining away. She watches from the doorway.

"I love Cheryl and I'm going to have her," says Don, six inches taller than Edward and several years younger.

"You won't keep her unless you've got plenty of money, you know. That's the only reason she's stayed with me so long. And she'll come right back to me when your funds run low." Edward's smile is tight and frigid.

"You won't be around any more," says Don in unconscious imitation of a B film heavy, as he tosses his glass at the wall and grabs at Edward's lapels.

"Don't be stupid. She isn't worth fighting over."

But his last three words are scarcely audible because Don's hands are round his throat now. Don's beautiful, virile hands fasten themselves around Edward's neck, with strong thumbs pressing in on either side of the windpipe. On the backs of his hands the veins and tendons are more pronounced than ever. Even the hairs seem to stand on end with effort. Edward's hands flap like a pair of doves. He tries to pull at Don's wrists but finds no strength in his desperation. Within seconds he loses consciousness and both men fall to the floor. Still Don maintains his grip, forcing life from Edward's body. Only after several more minutes does he rise. Cheryl runs across to embrace him, but he cannot look her in the eye.

Ah, yes, Cheryl thought, that's the way it was. In the end he found the determination to do it, and he even made a good job of disposing of the body. Professional pride, she thought.

But now, instead of lying dead on the pale green Wilton, Edward is sitting up, with thumb-prints vivid on his throat, staring accusingly at her.

"This was your doing," he says. "You pushed him into it." Edward's face fills her dream.

"You're being boring," she tells him. "In fact you often were boring." She decides to dream about something else, about something pleasant. She will dream about Don, who is a good, loving, thoroughly attentive husband to her, and in particular about his hands, which are no less exciting through familiarity than they were when she first met him.

She calls up his hands into view, but when they appear she feels a momentary stab of concern that they might be Edward's hands, because she can still see Edward's angry face behind them, fading yet just visible. Of course they are Don's hands, though. After all, isn't she controlling them? Aren't they part of her dream? The hands are so large and handsome, even larger than life. They reach out to her with the same loving gentleness as always, and their soft touch is like a kiss upon her breasts and thighs. She feels the strength, the power, the muscle behind that touch. Then the touch becomes a heavy weight, the caress a squeeze. The hands are gripping her now.

"Gently," she says. "Remember I'm a delicate flower."

The hands take no notice, so she sits up in bed and pushes at them. She dislodges them, but they move back towards her, clutching.

"No," she says, a little annoyed now. She flings back the quilt and swings her legs out of bed. Cold air strikes her body and she tries to pull her nightdress down to cover herself but it doesn't seem to be there at all. One hand grasps her shoulder. She stands up and shakes it off, but the other is flat against her belly. Naked, she runs round the end of the bed. The hands pursue her, flapping through the air like the wings of a large bat.

She screams in terror and jerks from side to side but the hands gain a firm hold on her neck. She can see Don still asleep in the bed and shouts out to him. He doesn't wake. The hands are very tight now.

She woke up to hear her cries echoing around the bedroom. Don was leaning over her, trying to offer comfort through the touch of his hand.

"I'm all right," she said thickly. "Just a dream." Then she turned over, away from her husband and his hands, seeking a return to peaceful sleep which she knew, somehow, would not come.

In the morning, when Don held her shoulders as he kissed her goodbye, she sensed that something had changed. She felt no tingle at his touch. That evening, as he sat reading the newspaper, she was able to study his hands unnoticed. Could it be that they were less attractive to her than formerly?

Her nightmare was repeated, not just once but on two, three, six successive nights. It broke down her defences, wore her out, left her looking pale and feeling old. By night his hands chased her, attacked her, mauling and bruising her body. By day she felt threatened by them, recoiling from his touch.

She could stand no more of it. He had not changed, and she loved him still, but his hateful hands had come between them. It was impossible for her to talk to him about it, and she wouldn't answer his plaintive questions.

No matter how often she went over it all in her mind there was only one course of action she could follow. She went to her doctor and persuaded him to prescribe a sedative—pheno- barbitone. That evening she crushed twelve of the tablets into Don's food, and he fell asleep at the table.

As they lay on the tablecloth his hands didn't look evil, but of course they were. They had committed murder, hadn't they? The kitchen cleaver was very sharp, and yet she found her task surprisingly difficult. She barely had the strength to finish, then she had problems staunching the flow of blood.

The first time they allow him to come and see her she runs to meet him at the door and kisses him on the mouth.

"I've missed you," she says. "I've missed you so much."

"Why did you do it?" he asks.

Chattering brightly she leads him to an unoccupied bench and sits beside him.

He says, "What use is a butcher without hands?"

By way of reply she quickly unwraps the coverings, exposing his stumps. "Stroke me," she says. "Touch me the way you used to."

Chris Morgan is a publisher's reader and teacher of creative writing to adults. His own non-fiction works have included Future Man: The Further Evolution of the Human Race, The Shape of Futures Past: The Story of Prediction *and, with Dave Langford,* Facts and Fallacies. *He is a major contributor to the* Illustrated Encyclopedia of Science Fiction *and has reviewed regularly for the science fiction magazines* Foundation *and* Vector. *Chris has also published a number of short stories and was runner-up in the 1984 Gollancz/Sunday Times science fiction competition. Presently he is editing* Dark Fantasies, *a big new anthology of subtle horror to be published next year by Century Hutchinson.*

A VISION OF REMBATHENE

Darrell Schweitzer

IT IS late at night, the feasting long over. Guttering torchlights swim in a haze of stale incense. The ghosts of ancient heroes, like shadows, stir in the corners, behind the limp hanging draperies and begin to move about as darkness creeps upon the exhausted court.

Amidst the revellers the King raises his head, and looks wearily over all. The Queen by his side whispers something into his ear, and he calls out to one on whom his eyes have come to rest, saying, "Tell me now of the cities of your dreams, that I too may behold them when I sleep."

The storyteller replies, "Of which, O King?"

"Of Rembathene."

"Ah Rembathene! Rembathene! Of all the cities revealed to me thou art the fairest! Rembathene, thy towers catch the dawn glow before even the mountain peaks the gods have wrought. Ah glorious Rembathene, a diamond with a thousand thousand facets, not built, but grown like some strange tree from that single pebble called The Soul of the Earth. Rembathene, all the Worlds envied thee!"

It was in Rembathene that Anahai the young king sat, on a throne of the East Wind carven, of night air frozen into a solid thing by magic and ancient rite, and shaped in secret beneath a broad moon of old, when they who first conceived Rembathene came out of the East armed with the sword. On this seat of his forebears he sat, brooding for the first time in the six months of his reign, the days of which before had dawned on nothing but peace and contentment, the enemies of his people having been subdued long before the birth of any man yet alive. Perhaps it was the very grace of his reign, and the splendor of his realm, that had brought him woe, for a pestilence had descended upon Rembathene, of the sort that a petty god sends when he is jealous.

By these signs was it known: First, a chill, such as one might feel when a window is left open in the evening, then a fever following, very slight, still not cause for alarm. But after that the suffering was swift and terrible. The afflicted one would awaken one morning covered with sores and welts, as if he had been flogged; blood would stream from every pore, and from his nose and ears; and he would go mad. In the end the flesh would decay while yet animate, and that which had once been a man would claw putrid chunks from itself as long as hands remained, and only after long hours of howling and writhing find relief at last in death. When a person was so stricken, all those around him would flee, for touch, or even nearness to such a one would mean contamination, and a similar fate within days. So the people of Rembathene and the lands around fled in all directions, into the city and out of it, from villages and towns into the fields, and from the fields into villages and towns. They trampled the crops they had planted. They clogged the roads. Many were crushed in the great arch of Rembathene which had been built for triumphant armies. And all this was to no avail, for when one of their number screamed and fell they could only turn in another direction, often back the way they had come. The sublety of the plague was that in any crowd there were always a few who were already infected but did not know it yet, so that Doom walked always as a silent companion among the refugees.

This young King, who knew himself to be the father of his people, who was willing to supplicate whatever god was angered and to sacrifice himself if need be, who had never truly proved to

And there in the doorway, with his scythe in one hand, his hourglass in the other, and his satchel of Years slung over his shoulder, the young King knew him. (Artist: Martin McKenna)

the people by effort that he was their king, listened helplessly to the reports brought to him, and watched much from his high windows. He felt in his heart the misery of the citizens of Rembathene.

He asked first of his Physician, "What cause?"

And the Physician answered, "Lord it is not known. Many and marvellous are the secrets of creation, and marvel enough would it be if a cure were to come to us, or some mitigation of our suffering. To know the cause is to ask too much."

He turned then to his Master of Leechcraft, saying, "Has your art been tried, to draw out the evil humors?"

"Aye, Majesty, and there are fewer of my brothers than there were before."

And to his Magician be said, "And magic?"

"Magic has been tried, O King, and there are today fewer magicians in the land than there are physicians or leeches."

Anahai ran his fingers nervously through his beard—it was not much, for his years were few—and the learned men stood impotent and afraid before him, and silence ruled in the room, until one spoke whose voice had not been heard before, an ancient who was not learned but wise, who had given up his name because he was so holy. All faced this revered one as he rose from where he had been seated, his black robe draped over him like a shroud, his polished ebony staff glistening like a living serpent.

"Most noble King," said he, "the cause of Rembathene's sorrow is not an imbalance of earthly humours, or a magical curse laid on the land by some enemy, or even the anger of a god, but this: beyond the world's rim there sits a Guardian with the Book of Earth in his lap, and this Guardian has fallen asleep with the Book open in his lap to the page of Rembathene, while be sleeps the spirit Nemesis has crept close, whispering 'Death, death, death' into the book."

"Then the Guardian must be awakened. How can this be done? What god shall I pray to?"

"There is one god only who can help you, one who is greater than all the gods of Earth. The God of Mysteries alone has power over the rim and beyond."

"He is not one to whom I sacrifice each day," said the King, puzzled. "Tell me of this god."

"Lord, there is little to say, for little is known. He resides in his tower, apart from the other gods, who are to him as ants to a great beast. He brushes them aside with a wave of his hand. His name cannot be known. His face cannot be seen. Perhaps he is, not a god at all, but Fate or Chance, or some other force not yet imagined, for his ways are mysterious and hidden from men."

"But how was he carven then, for surely his image was carven?"

The nameless man paused, then looked at the others about him and said, "This is a secret only the King may know."

The physician, the leech, the magician, and all the others were sent away, even the two massive eunuchs who stood perpetually on either side of the throne. Then when they were alone, the holy one continued.

"Know, O King, that of old a carver in Rembathene was touched by a madness, and his slaves took him to the top of the highest tower in the city, and they gave him his tools, and stone to work with, and they drew a curtain around him. For a month he carved, as the moon waxed and waned, and when the moon was gone he shrieked horribly, and staggered out, his face ashen and wide, and when his slaves beheld him they knew their duty, and slew him. They touched not the curtain, and none shall, until the ending of time, when one shall tear it back, look on the face of the God of Mysteries, and bring non-existence to all things."

"But if we cannot see his face, how can we know this nature? Is he cruel or kind? We cannot know if he mocks us."

"Even so, O King, for his ways are hidden from men."

"Still I must go to him. Where is his tower?"

"From a distance, it is seen by many. Close by, by a very few. Its base I touched for the first time in the fiftieth year of my contemplation, and I have gone there many times since. I can take another with me, for I have gained this strength."

At sunset, when the way he was to walk had been purified as far as ordinary men could follow it, King Anahai went with his guide through the streets of Rembathene, until they took a turn no others could take, and the city grew dim around them. They came at last to a tower glimpsed often by travellers who look back on Rembathene against the western sky, but seldom discerned by anyone else, and the King alone entered. He climbed a stairway of a hundred spirals, looking out windows at each turn, and saw the dark and quiet rooftops sink away below him; saw the sun burning low and golden, the purple on the horizon; and at last, when he neared the top, the stars appeared, seemingly below and round him, as if he had left the earth altogether.

He came finally to a room at the top of the tower, which the old man had described to him, wherein resided the god he sought. It was dark in there, dimly lit by tapers and without windows. The air was heavy with incense and dust and the stench of slaughtered offerings, making the place very holy. At the far end lay the crumbling skeleton of the mad carver, whose remains had never been touched, and beyond them was a curtain.

The King prostrated himself before the curtain, but presented no sacrifice, for when a ruler seeks rescue for his people from a god, the only thing he may offer is himself. Thus he rose empty handed to his knees and spoke humbly to the god, telling how the folk of his country had suffered, and begging that some cure to the disease be revealed.

Whatever was behind the curtain remained still. Anahai remained on his knees for many hours until his legs were numb, and still no answer came. He wanted very much to leave, but dared not, fearing the anger of the god, and hoping that the god was only thinking, and about to speak. Also he knew that if he were to leave, and return to his people without some solution, there would be no hope at all, and he would have failed in his duty. Kings who fail, he had always been taught, are seen in the corner of the eye as dim shapes which vanish when gazed upon directly. They are phantoms, wisps of smoke, sounds in the forest when no ear listens, unworthy to walk either on the earth or under the earth in the land of the dead.

The musty air made his eyes and his whole body heavy. He first sat back on his ankles, then brought his feet out from under him after a while and sat cross-legged. Later he slumped to the floor, asleep.

A dream came to him. He saw himself asleep in the tower, on the floor before the black curtain. Suddenly a wind blew the drape back, against the god, and there was a hint of an outline, a form hunched and powerful, and a face not at all like that of a man.

The figure on the floor screamed and thrashed about, yet there was no sound, and the spirit of Anahai, oddly detached and floating in the air overhead, knew that there was cause for terror, yet felt nothing. The body did not wake, and the dream continued. The lips of the idol moved and formed words silently, and in silence the body of the King got up and left the room. The spirit followed it down the hundred turns of the stair, into the city over which a heavy mist had fallen, through streets of looming, grey shapes, and out into the fields. Leagues passed, and at last a forest rose ahead, drenched in the fog so that the trees stood like dim Titans in the night. Led by a will not his own the King's body and awareness walked among them for a long way, somehow sure of the path no eye could make out.

Suddenly something before him moved, a shadow detaching itself from the general gloom to become a man.

"You!" cried the King. "Who are you?" As he spoke he awoke, and heard his voice echoing down the towers, "areyouareyouareyou...."

He was disoriented for a moment, but then he knew that the god had answered. He prostrated himself once more, in thanksgiving this time, before the curtain which was unruffled, and behind which no shape was visible, and he left the room. He looked out the first window he came to and saw that there was indeed a mist over the city, as he had dreamed, lapping against the towers like the silent waves of some magically conjured sea.

It was still the middle of the night. He was met in the darkness at the door of the tower by the holy man without a name, and with him he went through the faint, strangely turning streets until they emerged onto the pavement on which all men may walk. They went wordlessly back to the palace, where the King was met by his physician, his leech, and his wizard.

"Majesty, is it well?"

"I am sent to another place."

"Then go as a king must go, resplendent in your robes, with crown on your head and sword at your side, riding your finest stallion, with a troop of royal guards at your back."

And he did all these things, and rode out of the main gate of Rembathene, called the Mouth of the City, with his cavalry behind him, and his magician, his leech, and his physician at his side.

Also with him was the old man of mystical learning, who spoke to the king in strange signs, and in whispers none of the others could hear.

When they were more than a mile beyond the town, the mist had swallowed all the towers, Anahai turned to the horsemen and said, "I need you no longer," and sent them away, and the old man nodded.

After another mile he sent away the three who had advised him, saying to them also, "I need you no longer."

And when he came to the end of the wood he had seen in his dream he said to the wise man, "I need you no more either. From here I must go alone."

The one holy, beyond, naming, smiled. The King paused a second, unsure of himself and spoke once more.

"Know you to whom I am sent, or what price shall be asked?"

"No one knows that, save He who will not reveal it. He may have no price, or the world may be his price. He may jest and give forth nothing."

"Then goodbye," the King said, and he dismounted, handed the reigns of his horse to the other, and walked into the forest. His purple cloak, his red leggins, and his golden armour and crown seemed grey in the depths of the fog. He turned and looked back once and saw only an empty field. Far off he thought he heard hoofbeats on the muddy ground, then all was silent.

He entered the forest, and the mist hung over him like a damp blanket, and his steps were directed, as they had been in the dream. The trees loomed over him and vanished in the darkness above.

Then suddenly, as had been foretold, he met a stranger. One shadow detached itself from the rest and became a tall, thin man of fierce, weatherworn features, dressed in a cape the colour of the fog, and a tall peaked hat. His sudden motion startled the King.

"Who are you?" Again his voice echoed, but this time he did not wake.

The other did not answer, but stood again motionless, as if he were some strange and twisted tree that had seemed by some sorcery of mist and night to be momentarily alive.

"I am sent to you," said the King. "It has been revealed that I should meet you here by one who sits behind a curtain in the tower few can reach."

At that the stranger seemed to recognize him, and still not speaking, he motioned for the King to follow. Deeper into the woods they went, along a winding way the other knew. The stranger's cape hid him until at times Anahai feared he was alone, and lost, only to hear once more the soft, steady footsteps receding in front of him.

After a while the ground began to slope upward and the trees thinned out a little. They came to a gorge in which grey-black clouds broiled. A dwarf with a long spear challenged them with a savage yell, but the one who was leading cast a jewel as big as a fist over the head of the little man and into the pit. There was an explosion like the wrath of an angry god, and a bridge of ancient wood appeared. They crossed, and when they set foot on the other side the bridge vanished.

The trees got shorter and shorter, became gnarled and stunted little shrubs, then gave way to grass and moss, then to bare rock. The two climbed up precarious slopes, the fog clinging around them, as if the mountain wore it like a night-shirt. At last they came to the summit, and to a tiny hut. Inside was a bare table and two chairs. The stranger ushered the King in and motioned for him to sit.

Anahai looked around at the bareness of the dwelling.

"There is a pestilence in the land," he said doubtfully, "and I will give you anything you desire if—"

A long, flat box was placed on the table.

"Play this game with me."

Anahai nodded, and regretted he had spoken rashly. He knew to wait, to expect but not to ask, and hope that what he had requested to the God of Mysteries would be granted.

Inside the box was a notched board painted in black and white squares, and some glowing balls. With these they played a game, the King keeping balls on the white squares and the other keeping his on the black. When those of one were surrounded by those of the other, they were taken, and when the stranger captured one he placed it in his palm, and the light of it would go out, leaving it a dull brown. But when Anahai took one it would glow all the brighter. He won some and he lost some. Over this game the man in the grey cape showed emotion, gloating as he hoarded each new acquisition, scowling each time Anahai made one brighter. For a time the King feared he would not win, and played on with the resignation of a general fighting a hopeless battle in which he cannot surrender, but then the tide turned, and the room glowed with his winnings which he piled on one side of the table. It seemed to go on forever. Sometimes he felt as if he were asleep, and the motions of his hands were being made by the hands, independent of his will, and at times his mind was very clear, and he schemed and made strategies and practised diversions.

At last dawn came. The sun began to melt through the upper-most mist, and the gloom inside the hut was somewhat lessened. For the first time Anahai saw that there was a window. Through it he could see the dull orange glow of the morning, diffused in the fog.

He felt confused, exhausted, irritated at having spent the whole night doing this meaningless thing.

"What happens now?"

The other spoke for the second time. His voice was deep and hollow, as if coming from far away, from beyond the form that stood before Anahai.

"You have won. You hold more worlds than I."

"Will you then drive the pestilence away, if this is within your power?"

"Do? It shall be done! It is done! Know! Recognize! See, as was randomly pre-ordained!"

"See what? Recognize what?" The King's bewilderment was now mixed with terror.

The other made a sweeping gesture with his arms, his cloak flapping out like wings. He went to a corner, picked up two things, threw the door of the hut open and stood silhouetted, the rising sun behind him.

He smiled. For the first time Anahai noticed he had a long white beard.

"Do you not know me?"

And there in the doorway, with his scythe in one hand, his hourglass in the other, and his satchel of Years slung over his shoulder, the young King knew him.

In the middle of a day measured variously according to various calendars, one dressed in rich but ragged garments wandered into a village. He called all the people around him, and some came, while others went on about their business, and when they would not bow before him he grew angry, saying "I am your king! I am your king!" And he mentioned certain names, and the people laughed, and went away. He stood alone in their square until a very old woman came up to him and said she had heard those names before in tales told to her long ago, but that the place he spoke of had passed away ten times ten generations ago.

And on hearing this King Anahai began to weep, for he knew how his request had been fulfilled and who had done it, and he knew the answers to all the questions that had come into his head that morning, when he descended the mountain and found himself in a strange country. Somewhere the God of Mysteries was laughing perhaps, or perhaps not. Perhaps things could not have turned out any differently.

Time had driven the pestilence out of Rembathene.

Darrell Schweitzer's fantasy stories have been published in a number of magazines and anthologies, with recent appearances of his work in Rod Serling's Twilight Zone Magazine *and* Night Cry. *He is currently co-editor of the revived* Weird Tales *magazine as well as* Tales from the Spaceport Bar (Avon Books). *Starmont Books has recently published his essay-anthologies,* Discovering Modern Horror 2, *with others in the series forthcoming.* Pathways to Elfland, *a study of Lord Dunsany is due from Owlswick Press, while his fantasy serial* The White Isle, *originally published in* Fantastic (1980) *has been re-written for the book version due from* Weird Tales *Library.* Darrell's stories have previously appeared in *Fantasy Tales 6, 7 and 12 and we are pleased to welcome him back to our pages.*

WRITER'S CRAMP

David Riley

The Literary Editor of the *Digest of Horror* swung round lazily on his well-worn swivel chair as the morning's mail was brought in. Cartwright-Hughes looked askance down his long, thin, fastidious nose at the heap of battered manilla envelopes that were unceremoniously dumped in front of him by the office boy. Another batch of horrors, he thought languidly, and in more ways than one, no doubt! With a quiet sigh of resignation he picked out one of the slimmer envelopes, sliced it open down one edge with a blunt, bone-handled knife and extracted the enclosed batch of densely-typed sheets of paper. His teeth should twinge every time he received one of these, he thought as he surveyed the closely packed lines of typescript. The half dozen foolscap sheets were almost black with thick, smudgily typed letters. Lesson one for all would-be writers, he sermonised acidly, should be: always, but always type with two spaces at least between each line and just now and then, perhaps once every forty years or so, clean the keys of whatever decrepid, pre-adamite typewriter was being used. Really he shouldn't have to read something like this. It was appalling. Even the edges of the paper were furred from wear. But unfortunately—the Literary Editor's eternal bane!—the *Digest of Horror* was short as usual of publishable material and something would have to be found soon to fill the remaining eight

Cartwright-Hughes jerked his hand from the book in revulsion... (Artist: Jim Pitts)

pages in the March issue, which was due at the printers this week.

Cartwright-Hughes settled back as comfortably as his long spine would allow, propped his feet precariously on the edge of his desk and looked at the title heading of the story: *Paper Doom*. At least the title was reasonably original, he thought, pressing gamefully on. But his expectations quickly began to sink into a welter of unreadable Lovecraftian cliches—*bad* Lovecraftian cliches of the *worst* type. This was impossible! Yet, as his eyes scanned further lines, he had to concede that there was the germ, the merest germ of an idea in it. In some peculiar way the author's grasp of what he was writing about, clumsy though it may have been, did contain a dim air of authenticity. it was difficult for Cartwright-Hughes, who preferred his stories slick, to see just how this was being put over, yet it was there nevertheless.

Finally he flung the manuscript down onto the desk, surprised at himself for having ploughed stolidly all the way through it. Normally he would not have bothered to read more than a couple of pages of any story which was obviously unusable after the first two paragraphs. Reluctantly he had to admit that the basic plot was good but the writing, in almost inverse proportion, was horrifically bad. He pulled out a standard rejection slip from a drawer in his desk, clipped it to the manuscript and slid it into the stamped addressed envelope which the author had wisely supplied.

There the tale would have ended had it not been for the equally disappointing input of contributions to the *Digest of Horror* contained in the rest of the morning's mail. By noon Cartwright-Hughes was exasperated and tired. His eyes ached from deciphering the badly typed piles of manuscripts, some of which were blurred with coffee rings and other, less easily identifiable stains which made him wonder whether some of the putative authors had had sudden, short-lived fits of good taste before sending their manuscripts to him and temporarily made more appropriate use of them for mopping up the floor.

At 12.30 Sykes, the office manager, strolled in with a list of schedules. "*Digest of Horror* is getting awfully close to its deadline, old man," he intoned potentiously. He was a bald-headed Yorkshireman whose round spectacles seemed to reflect the light like spherical mirrors in a way which Cartwright-Hughes found mildly disconcerting.

Cartwright-Hughes tapped the pile of rejected manuscripts with his foot. "Literary merit seems to have escaped our hopefuls for the moment," he said, "though I suppose something might turn up in the second post."

"The last post will be more appropriate if it's not ready on time. This isn't the only magazine we've got to get ready for the newstands, you know, old man, nor is it our biggest money-maker these days from all accounts, eh?" This was a rather crude reference, delivered with typical Yorkshire bluntness by Sykes, to a sharp but, in Cartwright-Hughes' opinion, temporary slump in the sales of the *Digest*. "Market fluctuations," he had said breezily when tackled about it earlier, though he had felt an undeniable twinge of concern. Cartwright-Hughes yawned. "If the worst comes to the worst I could always write something myself to fill it out."

"Just so long as it's ready for Thursday," Sykes said. "That's the deadline, the *absolute* deadline. We can't wait any later than that."

By the end of the next day Cartwright-Hughes had taken to gnawing his thumbnails. Tuesday now, there was only one more day to go in which to get the *Digest* finished. To judge from the dismal calibre of amateurish contributions he had been inundated with for the past few months he had no illusions as to what to expect in tommorow's post. It was like that poem by Yeats, he thought:

"The best lack all conviction, while the worst
Are full of passionate intensity."

There was only one thing for it, he thought reluctantly as he gazed gloomily at the secretarial staff in the general office through the dusty windows of his own sanctum sanctorum, and that was to dash something off himself. It would mean having to burn some of the proverbial midnight oils unfortunately, but there did not seem to be any realistic alternative. He could, he supposed, have used an old, out-of-copyright reprint, perhaps something from Poe or Bierce, but the *Digest of Horror* was basically a magazine of contemporary fiction. The larger than normal number of old reprints over the past few months had almost certainly been the main reason for the magazine's drop in sales. The task now was to win back its readership. More reprints wouldn't do that. Far from it!

No, there was no other feasible choice. He would have to write something himself.

But what?

Cartwright-Hughes let his fertile imagination amble back over plots he had come across amongst the dirge of unprintable material submitted to the *Digest* recently. Perhaps there was something amongst these which could be quickly chiselled into some kind of presentable shape, but it was usually the hackneyed plots of the contributions that had them scuttering back through the post to their authors with rejection slips tagged to their tails rather than just poor or inferior writing. Imagination and, in particular, originality were the things they mainly lacked. Yet there was one recently which he seemed to remember having been impressed with at the time, though its lamentably bad writing had earned it a well-deserved rejection slip.

Abruptly he reached across his desk for the typewriter, tugging it towards him with a triumphant grunt. *Paper Doom* had had a plot he could use, up-dated with a few amendments and additions. The bare bones of its plot would do nicely for the kind of filler he wanted, though he would have to change its title.

With practised ease Cartwright-Hughes' fingers tapped out the title at the head of a clean sheet of A4 paper; *Hand-pressed*, he'd call it, in reference to the affliction the main protagonist in the story would literally have cursed upon him.

The story, which was reasonably straight forward, concerned a man's revenge against his wife's lover. Here Cartwright-Hughes diverged radically from the original story, but *Digest of Horror's* most popular items often figured tales of gruesome, matrimonial revenge, sometimes, though not always by any means, involving the supernatural. The emphasis was strictly on *horror* and plenty of blood, digestible or otherwise.

The method of revenge was the only real act of plagiarism involved although Cartwright-Hughes did not feel guilty of even this. After all, he thought defensively, the original story was unpublishable anywhere.

Sticking to the original theme of *Paper Doom* the vengeful husband, who is depicted as having an academic knowledge of certain forbidden "Black Arts", sends an old book on demonology to the unsuspecting seducer. On opening the book the man's attention is drawn to a short phrase on the first page which has been written in what looks like brown ink. The ink, of course, is blood. This is the key which immediately unleashes the terrible nemesis which has been sent to him. The page is not paper at all but some kind of thin, leathery substance disturbingly akin to tanned human skin. No sooner has the man read the inscription to himself than the page suddenly starts coming to "life", wrenching itself free from the binding of the book and hurling itself at the man's right hand, which it completely envelopes. So tight does it cling to him that it seems more like an undersized leather glove—or as if his own hand had suddenly aged into the claw of an ancient corpse.

The repulsive skin cannot, he discovers to his horror, be removed nor can it be seen by anyone else, as if it was there only in his own imagination. But the real horror comes when he finds that, not only has his hand, in his own eyes at least, been hideously disfigured by the raddled, corpse-like skin, but whenever he is not in complete control of it his hand can unexpectedly act with an apparent will of its own—a will which it soon becomes clear is determined upon his destruction.

The culmination of the story, aimed unerringly at as gruesome a climax as possible, comes when the unfortunate seducer discovers that the only way in which he can rid himself of the curse is to turn it back on its creator. This, sticking again to the plot of *Paper Doom*, is achieved by the victim reciting backwards the original phrase which brought the page to "life" and severing his hand from his wrist with one chop of a machete. This drives the demoniacal skin back onto its creator, whose throat is ripped out in a ghastly welter of blood.

With the final gory paragraphs completed Cartwright-Hughes heaved the typewriter back across the desk with a sigh of contentment—a *tired* sigh of contentment. It was now 12.15 a.m., but at least the *Digest of Horror* could go to press complete. And Sykes would have nothing to grumble about for another month.

To Cartwright-Hughes' satisfaction there were no more hitches in the March issue of the *Digest*. Eventually, as sales figures started to come in, they even showed a slight but significant upwards climb, confirming for him his diagnosis for its recent slump. From now on, God willing, there would be no more reprints from the "mouldy oldies", as one irate reader had referred to them, but brand new, garish, matrimonial bloodbaths, of the type which the *Digest*'s readership apparently lapped up with enthusiasm—but then Cartwright-Hughes had never had any great respect for the readership of the *Digest of Horror*. As he had once expressed it to a colleague: "Always presume that your average reader is about twelve years old, spotty, sadistic and partially illiterate, and you can't go far wrong."

Less than a week later he received a small, buff envelope in the post addressed to him by name. To his surprise he found that it was from the author of *Paper Doom*. Cartwright-Hughes read it silently to himself, his face growing pale. Finally he jerked back in his chair and swore. "Cheeky bastard!" he exploded indignantly.

"Anything the matter, old man?" Sykes, who had been strolling past the office when Cartwright-Hughes gave vent to his outburst, poked his head through the doorway. Cartwright-Hughes waved the hand-written letter towards him angrily. "This cheeky son of a bitch is accusing me of stealing his story!"

"And did you?"

Cartwright-Hughes snorted. "The damn thing was that badly written he couldn't have given it away, never mind have it stolen. The worst I did was to use a couple of his ideas in the last issue of the *Digest*. And ideas aren't copyright, whatever this nut might think to the contrary. He should have felt flattered that I'd used them. At least when I'd finished they were readable, which is more than could be said about the gibberish he wrote." Cartwright-Hughes reached into his breast pocket for a handkerchief to wipe away the spittle from his lips.

"Write back to him then and put him in his place," Sykes said. "If you're right in what you say he hasn't a leg to stand on."

Cartwright-Hughes grunted. He had already decided to do this anyway. As Sykes ambled down the general office, shaking his head, Cartwright-Hughes lunged for his typewriter, angry phrases smouldering through his mind. The man had almost threatened him, he thought indignantly. Threatened! He'd see who threatened who. When it came to cutting phrases there was one thing being an amateur and quite another thing being a professional, and

Cartwright-Hughes hadn't got where he was without learning a trick or two.

Cartwright-Hughes glanced at the address on the letter:

A.J. Dymchurch, Esq.,
The Laurels,
Watery Lane,
Oswaldtwistle,
Lancashire.

Well, Mr. Dymchurch, Cartwright-Hughes thought harshly, we'll now see what you're made of. His fingers dived aggressively at the keys on his typewriter, venting his feelings in a machine-gun-like clatter of invective. The cheek of the man had been unbelievable. To demand—to actually demand—that he publish an apology in the next issue of the *Digest of Horror* for stealing his story! Cartwright-Hughes growled between clenched teeth. And then, adding insult to injury, to warn him of the consequences if he didn't in vague and bewildering terms like he did! Any psychiatrist, given that letter, would have had the poor fool locked up. Cartwright-Hughes' fingers quickly typed out this point, ending with an explosive exclamation mark which almost broke the key from the typewriter.

"Put this in the first post," he called out to the office boy as he meandered aimlessly past, throwing the letter, now signed, sealed and addressed, across to him. "First class post." That would show that he meant business!

To Cartwright-Hughes' satisfaction the next couple of weeks were spent peacefully on holiday. When he eventually returned to the office, happy, relaxed and suntanned after a much needed break in the Austrian Alps, he found a pile of mail on his desk. "Good grief,' he muttered as he disdainfully looked over the parcels of manuscripts. He pulled one out. This must contain a novel at the very least, he thought as he weighed its heavy bulk in his hands. It was hardly worth the effort of opening it since the *Digest of Horror*, as everyone should know by now, he thought, never used anything longer than a ten thousand word novelette. Shaking his head Cartwright-Hughes cut the parcel open to see if return postage had been enclosed. To his surprise he found that the parcel didn't contain a typescript at all but a hardbound book. 'What on earth was all this about?' he wondered as he pulled it out.

Clearing the rest of the mail to one side he rested the volume on his desk. It was very old and rather ugly; its wrinkled binding looked as if damp had at one time or another taken a firm grip of it and ravaged it with decay. A thick, noxious odor rose mustily from it. After touching it he carefully and fussily wiped his fingers clean on a handkerchief of the clammy feeling the book's cover had coated them with. Something about this disturbed him but he could not figure out what . . . or why. Perhaps it was the smell, which was as if some small animal had crawled into the book and died.

Cartwright-Hughes flipped the book open to see if there was anything tucked away inside to indicate who had sent it. It was then, quite suddenly, that warning bells—or their mental equivalent—went off inside his head. He knew, instinctively, without any shadow of a doubt, that he must not look at the page facing him, but it was already too late. His eyes were almost compulsively drawn to the dark red letters scrawled across it:

Mutato nomine de te fabula narratur."

Change the name and the tale is about you? Cartwright-Hughes' fingers briefly touched the jagged writing to smooth the paper, which had begun to wrinkle oddly. As he did so there was a sudden ripple of motion across it and the start of a tear appeared at one end. Cartwright-Hughes jerked his hand from the book in revulsion but the page came with it. Like a tattered, wind-blown moth the parchment flapped about his hand. It was stuck, as if glued to his fingers. Vainly he shook his hand to throw the thing from him but the wrinkled parchment clung tenaciously to him, enfolding itself about his hand. Cartwright-Hughes knew that this was ridiculous. It was as if he had blundered into that trite story he had had so much trouble about. But stories like that never happened, not in real life! He clutched, frantically at the page to tear it from him but as he pulled it was like trying to rip his own skin from his hand. He cried out in pain and fell back, bewildered, against his desk, slipping to the floor where he wrestled with the thing, but it seemed to have him trapped in an iron vice moulded to the exact shape of his hand. And the vice was tightening. Crushed, his fingers were already starting to go numb. No! *Noooo!* He grunted with exertion but his fingers could do nothing against the hideous, fleshy parchment that had trapped them.

For a moment Cartwright-Hughes, who was not a strong man, felt dizzy and he knew that he was falling into a faint. When he recovered moments later he saw a circle of faces staring down at him.

"Are you all right, old man?" Sykes asked as he pushed a folded jacket beneath his head. "Take it easy. Don't rush to get up."

Cartwright-Hughes breathed deeply. He had passed out, that was all, he thought. Overwork probably. A feeling of relief passed over him. It had, after all, been nothing worse than a nightmare as he lay sprawled on the floor!

Slowly Sykes helped him to his feet while someone fetched a chair. As he sat down Cartwright-Hughes glanced at his hands.

"Is anything wrong?" Sykes asked; he gripped Cartwright-Hughes' shoulders to steady him, certain that he was about ready to collapse again. But Cartwright-Hughes rallied himself, though he remained silent for the moment as the full horror of it all started to sink in. He knew that there was no point in saying anything now, not now, because no one, no one but himself, would ever be able to see it. He stared in horrified silence at the wrinkled "glove" that covered his hand like a membrane of ancient skin.

When he finally felt strong enough to stand up he asked Sykes if he would drive him home. "Anything to oblige, old man," Sykes responded with the kind of over-enthusiasm people often adopt towards those they consider invalids. Subduing the irritation he would have normally reacted to this with Cartwright-Hughes walked with him to the car park. Sykes' amiable if aimless chatter passed him unheard as he pondered on the situation he now found himself in. Every moment or so he glanced at his hand as if hoping that eventually he would find that there was nothing there and that it had all be an hallucination after all, but the wrinkled skin was there every time, and he knew, deep down, that this was no hallucination. It was real. Horribly, horribly real!

He thought back over the plot of *Paper Doom*. He had no doubts as to the source of the thing that had afflicted him. A.J. Dymchurch, Esq., he was the man. He was the man all right, the dirty, vindictive . . .! Cartwright-Hughes drew his lips back taut across his teeth in a fit of fury. Yet at the same time a grim chill of foreboding crept through him as he looked back over the story he had partially purloined. As Sykes turned the ignition in his heavy Wolseley saloon and drove them out onto the busy main road, heading towards St. Johns Wood, Cartwright-Hughes wondered whether the rest of the "curse" as depicted in Dymchurch's story would follow, in particular the determination of his disfigured hand to kill him. He stared distrustfully at it. While he was in concious control of it he knew he was safe, but how could he possibly keep this up all the time? It was impossible and he knew it. Yet, would he have to go to the violent extreme depicted in the story to free himself of it? He shuddered nauseously at the thought. A squeamish man at the best of times when faced with reality he found the whole idea inconceivable.

Sykes left him outside the entrance to the select block of flats in which he lived. As he hurried in the doorman called out: "Just one letter today, sir." Thanking him, Cartwright-Hughes accepted it from him and hastened to the lift. He clutched the small, buff envelope in his left hand, having developed a sudden aversion to using the other "contaminated" hand for anything, especially this; one glance at the crabbed handwriting on the front of the envelope was enough to inform him of the identity of the sender.

Safely back in his flat, with its broad view of St. Johns Wood, Cartwright-Hughes poured himself a strong gin and tonic and put a record on the music centre, choosing a favourite Mozart concerto to help ease the tension that had gripped him and to restore at least the semblance of some kind of normality. Gripping the gin gratefully he settled back in an armchair by the window and carefully unsealed the letter.

"Dear Mr. Cartwright-Hughes," it read, "You will have by now received the book I sent to you, and taken possession of the page enclosed in it. After the way in which you criminally stole the story I sent to you I doubt whether you are uncertain of what will happen next. You have been warned once already. That should have been enough. Yet I am not a heartless man. There is still time. If you carry out what I set out in my previous letter to you I can reverse what has happened. But time is short. And growing shorter. I must have your reply, in writing, soon or it will be too late. Yours, etc., A.J.D."

Cartwright-Hughes sank back despairingly in the armchair. He knew that he was faced with an insoluble problem. How could he possibly confess publicly to having stolen another writer's story? Not only would that mean his professional ruin but, even more importantly perhaps, it would make him a laughing stock from now on with everyone he knew. It was downright impossible for him to do anything like this. Impossible! He might just as well as cut his own throat. There was no way in which he could expose himself like that, whatever the cost.

Abruptly he jumped to his feet, put away the gin and strode into the study in the next room where he unlocked the writing bureau in which he kept his personal mail and laid out a clean sheet of paper. Drawing up a chair he started to write out a reply to Dymchurch, a reply that was radically different to the one he had sent to him before. As he wrote he avoided as much as possible looking at the wrinkles and creases of dried skin that covered his hand. Instead he concentrated on trying to write something conciliatory to Dymchurch, something which would enable him to avoid the personal and professional suicide of confessing to plagiarism. Ideas floated through his mind as he wrote. An offer of money—a substantial offer of money—was one. Another was the offer of a series of stories in future issues of the *Digest*, although that was certain to send sales plummeting to an all time record low. Play on his vanity, he thought cynically. That was the thing. If Dymchurch could go to the extremes he had in revenge for him taking a couple of ideas from his story the man must have an obsessive ego. He must have.

Cartwright-Hughes paused to trace back over what he had written. As he glanced at the letter his face became deathly pale and a tremor started to pulse in his lower lip.

"Don't waste your time pathetically pleading. The terms have been stated. Either accept or face the consequences. There is no other choice."

Cartwright-Hughes stared at the crabbed handwriting bewilderedly. His right hand felt even more alien to him now than before. It wasn't his at all any more. It was possessed, *stolen*!

He picked up a paper knife and gently tried to prise the "skin" away but it was no use. The thing wouldn't budge except if he cut his own skin away at the same time. Was that the solution then? Get some back street surgeon to cut the skin, both skins, from his hand? If he did that, though, he might just as well have his hand cut off since he doubted if so much skin could be replaced through skin grafts. He might be better off, then, having his hand amputed, properly carried out under anaesthetic by a surgeon. At least that way it would be painless. But he couldn't just go to any ordinary surgeon for a job like that. He'd more likely end up being certified by any reputable doctor. The only kind he could approach would be someone who had been struck off, someone crooked.

Fortunately Cartwright-Hughes had his contacts, built up over the years from his involvement at one time with cocaine sniffing. Erosion of the nasal passages due to "snorting" the stuff resulted in the not unusual necessity of having to have plastic surgery performed on his nose. Since cocaine was illegal he had had to take the prudent step of arranging through a "friend of a friend" to have the operation performed in a discrete clinic somewhere in Brixton. He remembered the anonymous looking red-brick tenement where the squall of Reggae drowned the screams of untended babies in the surrounding slums. Although he didn't know the "surgeon's" name he was told at the time by his contact that the man had once been highly placed in his field until struck off for unethical and somewhat immoral practices.

Cartwright-Hughes thumbed through his personal phone book, then dialed. Half an hour later an appointment had been made for that evening. He still felt sick in the pit of his stomach at what he had to undergo, but there was no choice. He flexed his fingers. It was almost inconceivable that anything had really changed. It still felt like his own hand. It still felt under his control. But the wrinkled skin sheathing it and the alien writing on the notepaper were clear enough proof that his hand had been possessed. He dared not wait for it to act unexpectedly against him, as he knew it eventually would, to bring about his death. It was like walking about with an assassin attached to the end of his arm.

When, later that day, he ordered a taxi to take him to Brixton for his appointment Cartwright-Hughes vowed to himself that somehow, in some way he would get his revenge. However clever he might think he was Dymchurch would not get away with this.

The diesel train drew up at the station where it was instantly battered by blasts of rain. Cartwright-Hughes glimpsed a dispiritingly small, untended platform through the dirt-smeared window of the carriage door as he tugged it open. A plain sign read: *Church and Oswaldtwistle*. He shivered as he stepped down onto the platform at the cold, penetrating winds and clutched his briefcase to him like a shield in his left hand as he hurried to the steps which brought him down to Union Road. An old man, the flat cap on his head bowed down against the rain like a battering ram, was shuffling past. Cartwright-Hughes called out, asking the way to Watery Lane. The old man looked at him with glassy, red-rimmed eyes.

"That'll be up the'er," he pointed waveringly. "Tha goes past t'Library. Tha sees it? Then tha turns reet, keep on goin' till tha comes t' th'end. Then keep on goin' to tha left." He rambled on a few more directions which Cartwright-Hughes carefully noted.

"Thank you. Thank you very much," he said.

"Think nowt on it."

Cartwright-Hughes thought for a moment, then said: "I don't suppose you know someone up that way called Dymchurch, do you?"

The old man cocked his head to one side and looked at him shrewdly. "Albert Dymchurch?"

"It could be. I only know his initials: A.J."

"Aye, that'll be 'im. Albert Joseph Dymchurch." He spat eloquently into the gutter. "If'n I were you I'd steer clear o' that on'. Should 'a' bin locked up years ago."

"Why?"

"*Why?* 'Cause 'iz brains are adled, that's why. Always 'ave bin." He grinned confidentially. "If you're 'ere to certify 'im you'll no' go short o' volunteers to back up what I say. Iz that what you're 'ere for?"

Cartwright-Hughes hesitated, uncertain now whether under the circumstances he had been wise to let anyone know that he was here to see Dymchurch, especially a garrulous old man like this. There were certain to be plenty of questions asked later and the less anyone knew about him the better.

Noticing his hesitation the old man chuckled good-naturedly. "Don't worry yoursen, lad. I'll not press you ifn' you don't want to say nothin'. I respects a man 'as'll keep a secret. Too much loose talk these days az it iz. But if'n you are 'ere to lock th'owd blighter up then you've got my blessin's lad. Aye, that you 'ave, all reet."

Following the old man's directions as the wind and rain gradually died down from being vilely unpleasant to a kind of persistent dreariness, Cartwright-Hughes came some fifteen minutes later to a narrow lane leading onto Oswaldtwistle Moors. A small terraced cottage faced him there, its neighbours blatantly derelict. Dead ivy covered its stone walls like dried varicose veins. A musty smell of unwashed linen, cats and other domestic animals hung round the door, indication enough of how it would smell inside. There were no curtains at the windows, only discoloured newspapers held in place by crinkled strips of equally discoloured sellotape. On the unpainted, splintered and damp-swollen door was a small plaque, "The Laurels" pretentiously painted across it in crumbling "Olde English" letters.

Cartwright-Hughes rapped officiously on the door and tried to adopt the stance appropriate to a local council official. This, he thought, would give him the best means of gaining entry into the house without rousing any undue suspicions. Brow-beat the bastard first, he thought, with a load of domineering bull-shit— sanitation and hygiene, appropriately enough, were obvious targets he could use. Then . . .!

There was a muffled creak at the door, quickly followed by another, though neither had any noticeable effect. A further creak followed, impatiently this time, and the door was suddenly tugged open. It jammed just as suddenly on the uneven flagstones inside, leaving a gap just wide enough to squeeze through. The odour of unwashed linen and animals became appreciably stronger and was joined by a further smell of cooking—this appeared to consist mainly of some kind of boiled vegetable, probably cabbage, though Cartwright-Hughes was by no means certain.

"Yes?"

An elderly, narrow-shouldered man in a threadbare cardigan peered round the doorway. His thin, angular, unshaven jaws were clamped tight, tensely, while his pale grey, rather watery eyes scrutinized Cartwright-Hughes through slightly misshapen horn-rimmed spectacles perched at an odd angle on the bridge of his nose. Tiny tufts of greyish hairs sprouted like a kind of sparse, miniturised sedge from the tip of his nose and the lobes of his reddish ears, accentuating his definitely unkempt appearance.

"Mr. Dymchurch?" Cartwright-Hughes enquired, briefcase held tight against his abdomen in bureaucratic fashion. "Mr. Albert Dymchurch?" he added pedantically.

"Ye-es." Apprehensively he glanced at the briefcase much as a downtrodden Roman citizen might have looked upon the *fasces* of a Senatorial magistrate.

Despite the hatred and anger which had driven him here all the way from London, Cartwright-Hughes realised that he was now beginning to enjoy himself, yes, despite *everything*.

"I've been asked to see you," he said, "to check your sanitation. There have been complaints . . ."

Dymchurch stepped back into the house. "Please come in, please come in," he said, ineffectively tugging at the door to widen the gap. "I shall 'ave to get this fixed some day," he muttered apologetically as Cartwright-Hughes squeezed through the doorway and followed him into the dim room beyond.

Confusion and dust lay all about him in the living room—or whatever Dymchurch chose to term it. An old fashioned sideboard cluttered with books that looked equally old; an open coal fire from which a few sickly looking flames periodically spluttered; several amrchairs, of which all but one were covered with piles of still more books; and a 1950's style bicycle propped against one wall, while above the fire place there hung a framed portrait in oils of a thin-faced man with a yellowish complexion and slightly protuberant eyes. The whole room filled Cartwright-Hughes' fastidious soul with revulsion—a revulsion born from the dreary, defeated squalour of it all. Dymchurch stood watching him, his baggy trousers and patched cardigan so in place amongst the upheaval that it almost acted as a kind of camouflage for him, blending him into the background. Cartwright-Hughes studied this man who had hated him so much as to do what he had done to him. He looked too ineffectual, too old, too decrepit, like a worn-out and senile schoolteacher, to have done all of that.

Dymchurch waited patiently for him to speak.

There was no point now in any further prevarication. Cartwright-Hughs, looking down on Dymchurch from an advantage of an additional six inches, said: "We've never met before but you know me. At least you know me enough to have tried to have me killed."

Dymchurch's eyes opened wide, apprehensive again and perhaps just a little afraid. His hands fluttered uncertainly to his lips as he spoke. carefully choosing his words. "You are, I take it, from London—not the council?"

Cartwright-Hughes admitted the obvious, "Cartwright-Hughes is the name," he said, unclipping his briefcase. He thumped the heavy book he had been sent onto the floor. Spurts of dust erupted from beneath it, fogging the light from the windows. He reached into his briefcase again and brought out a small package wrapped in oilskins. In carrying out all of these actions he used only his left hand. His right arm was used solely to hold the brief-case pressed to his stomach. Suddenly he let the briefcase drop to the floor and held his arm towards Dymchurch, revealing the stump that terminated at his wrist. The flesh was still covered with gauze from the operation. A dark stain tinged it.

Dymchurch clucked. His eyes peered speculatively at Cartwright-Hughes. He was plainly surprised.

Cartwright-Hughes held the oilskin package to his chest and picked it open. Inside lay a wrinkled hand, *his* hand, his *stolen* hand. He threw it down at Dymchurch's feet.

"You know what will happen next." he said.

Dymchurch shrugged. "Whatever will be . .," he murmured. "I can do nothing to stop you, not now." He shrugged carelessly. Cartwright-Hughes noticed for the first time a steely glint in the man's otherwise watery eyes. Was that indicative of the harder, tougher part of the man, that part that had given him the will to delve as deeply as he had into whatever forbidden knowledge he had chosen to master?

Cartwright-Hughes straightened his back. "The tables are turned now and you can learn what it is like to be cursed. And learn how careless you were to use the same curse against me as you used in your story." Cartwright-Hughes opened a slip of paper, from which he read: "*Narratur fabula te de nomine mutato!*"

Dymchurch stepped back as the wrinkled skin covering the severed hand started to move. It seemed to heave itself up from the hand and Cartwright-Hughes could see the red perforations beneath where it had clung, leach-like, to his flesh. Like a deformed moth the "skin" flapped itself and rose unsteadily into the air. it was then that Cartwright-Hughes began to suspect that something was wrong. For a start off Dymchurch had developed a tight, little, satisfied smile which threatened momentarily to grow. Why? But worse, he saw that the "skin" was starting to move, not towards Dymchurch, but towards himself.

Cartwright-Hughes stumbled back, falling over the arm of the chair behind him. The "skin" suddenly leaped forward. Instinctively he brought up the stump of his right arm to shield his face from it, but the thing wrapped itself about his wrist for the merest moment, biting into the only partially healed wound, then slithered past, flapping towards his face. "Why?"Cartwright-Hughes cried out in bewilderment. "Why?" The "skin" slapped into his face. Where its abrasive underside touched him it left bright red weals that trickled blood. He clutched at it with his left hand but the perforations beneath it seemed to burn his fingers as if it was covered with thousands upon thousands of tiny, venomous mouths that sucked at him. He rolled over as it tightened itself about his throat, as the room began to spin about his head and the air seemed to boom inside his ears. "Why? Why?" he choked, his words all by undistinguishable as the "skin" tightened its grip and blood spurted in hundreds of tiny jets from beneath it.

Dymchurch strolled curiously over as Cartwright-Hughes collapsed convulsively onto the floor. His face was purple now above the livid "skin" wrapped about his throat and small, bubbling, mewling sounds were all that escaped from his lips, which were drawn back agonisingly from his teeth. Dymchurch smiled as the Literary Editor's feet kicked out ineffectually, weakening quickly.

It was fortunate, Dymchurch thought, that he had not stuck to fact all the way through the story he had submitted to the *Digest of Horror* otherwise Cartwright-Hughes would never have tried, without the protection of a pentagram about him, to order a gaunt back to its inhospitable world between the plains. They became terribly, even nastily aggressive about things like that. "But you should have known," Dymchurch said reprovingly to the shuddering remains of Cartwright-Hughes, whose swollen eyes had already started to cloud over, "that there is the world of difference between fact and fiction and the two should never be confused. You of all people should have known better than that."

David Riley *has been writing fiction for a number of years and has had stories published in such anthologies and magazines as* Death, *the* 11th Pan Book of Horror, Year's Best Horror Stories I, New Writings in Horror 1 *and* 2, World of Horror, Whispers, Dark Horizons *and* The First World Fantasy Awards. *One of his tales, 'The Satyr's Head', which was the title story of an anthology edited by David Sutton for Corgi Books, is now included within the text of a novel of the same name and continues the horrific theme of that story. Two further novels,* Cursed Be the Ground *and* The Talent *(a psychic thriller), are in the pipeline.*

THE CLOVEN CROSS
Chris Naylor

Under a pale moon, on a dark hill,
Stands a cleft cross of weatherworn stone;
Hewn out by wind and storm, graven by time—
Raised, lost, found, feared, left alone.

Eastward lifts one arm, westward the other,
Signing some way long forgotten.
Moss creeps across its grey foot—over wood
Once a pedestal, now riddled rotten.

Lore gives no clue, legend no tale,
Telling its use or true age;
Years run to lifetimes—it stands little changed
While man and the elements rage.

Under a dark sky, on a high hill,
Figures of shadow and light
Fleet past the forked cross like phantoms, half-seen,
And vanish again in the night.

MEMORIES

Robert E. Howard

Shall we remember, friend of the morning,
Dusk of the twilight and rose of the dawn?—
Laughing we fared in our youthfullness, scorning—
Mornings as golden shall lift when we're gone.

Oceans are eld and the mountains are hoary
Ancient forgetfulness leaves them apart,
We shall remember out youth and the glory
We breathed when out race was just at its start.

Soon shall we fade as the twilight's red splendour
Fades to the misting of magical dusk
Soon to the eons our souls shall surrender ·
Ghosts dim at twilight, a faint breath of musk.

We shall remember, our ghosts shall remember
Sunsets of glory and pale rose of dawn;
We shall remember, our ghosts shall remember
Ages and ages long after we're gone.

THE CAULDRON

Welcome to the new-look *Fantasy Tales* Britain's paperback
magazine of fantasy and terror! If this is the first time
you've ever heard of us, then we should point out that *Fantasy
Tales* has been around for quite some time—in fact, at the beginning of 1988 we celebrated our tenth anniversary . . . But up until
now the magazine has been published semi-professionally, one
of a number of 'small press' journals that proliferate in the field
of fantasy, horror and science fiction.

The first issue of *Fantasy Tales* appeared in 1977, and at the
time it was specifically designed to meet the need for a regular
magazine outlet for stories and artwork in the fantasy and horror genre. It was decided to make the magazine a visual tribute
to the old 'pulp' magazines of the 1930s and '40s, and *Fantasy
Tales* recreated the style and entertainment value which had
marked the success of such legendary pulp magazines as *Weird
Tales*. On a very small budget and a limited print-run we turned
out nearly a score of issues, bringing to readers many old and
new writers (some of whom had been original contributors to
Weird Tales), embellished by some of the most talented fantasy
illustrators around.

Fantasy Tales has won the British Fantasy Award seven times,
and is a recipient of the prestigious World Fantasy Award. Several
of the stories we have published have themselves been nominees
and award winners in the BFA and WFA short story category,

with a number of tales being subsequently reprinted in annual 'Year's Best' anthologies and major collections. Our contributors over the years have included Clive Barker, Ramsey Campbell, Robert Bloch, H.P. Lovecraft, Fritz Leiber, Charles L. Grant, Dennis Etchison, Brian Lumley, Manly Wade Wellman, Karl Edward Wagner and H. Warner Munn amongst many others. All the above-mentioned authors are currently featured in *The Best Horror from Fantasy Tales* (Robinson Publishing, £11.95), a hardcover anthology which showcases a selection of the best stories from past issues of the magazine.

You can subscribe to the magazine at the amazingly low rate of £3.60 for four issues, which is a bargain considering it means that you will not have to comb the streets looking for the latest issue. If you live overseas you can subscribe for £7.60 or $14.00 for four issues and be sure of getting every new issue by airmail. Please send all subscription enquiries to Robinson Publishing at 11 Shepherd House, Shepherd Street, London W1Y 7LD, UK.

However, with our re-launch in the new paperback-style format, it is time for *Fantasy Tales* to look forward to the future: the contemporary design and increased distribution outlets should give us a wider readership and an opportunity to present even more authors—both old and new—to those who enjoy stories of the macabre and fantastic. Remember, *The Cauldron* is *your* column—we want to hear what you think of our new image, which stories and artwork you enjoyed best and, perhaps most importantly, what you would like to see in future issues . . .

In *FT* we don't have long editorials, but there are a few things we'd like to mention this issue: elsewhere we have paid tribute to Lin Carter, who was a major force in fantasy fiction and a contributor to the magazine. And we must also mention the death earlier this year of Randall Garrett, whose *Just Another Vampire Story* appeared in our fifth issue. Garrett was a science fiction writer perhaps best known for his supernatural sleuth, Lord Darcy. These stories, set in a world where magic really works, were chiefly published in the SF digest magazines and later collected in three books, *Too Many Magicians*, *Murder and Magic* and *Lord Darcy Investigates*. More recently, Darcy's exploits have been continued by writer Michael Kurland in *Ten Little Wizards* (Ace Books).

Some other books *FT* readers might like to look out for this autumn include Bantam's *Prime Evil*, a major anthology of original horror stories, edited by Douglas E. Winter, and featuring an impressive line-up that includes Stephen King, Peter Straub, Whitley Strieber, Clive Barker, Dennis Etchison, Ramsey Campbell and M. John Harrison. Etchison's second major collection of short stories, *Red Dreams*, is out from Futura, while from Gollancz comes Robert Holdstock's long-awaited sequel to his World Fantasy Award-winning novel *Mythago Wood*, title *Lavondyss*. And Holdstock joins Christopher Evans to edit *Other Edens 2* from Unwin Hyman, another superb anthology of the best of British speculative writing. Stephen King fans will want *The Gunslinger*, the first in his post-apocalyptic fantasy series from Sphere or, if you prefer your fantasy on the lighter side, you could do worse than check out Craig Shaw Gardner's hilarious *A Multitude of Monsters* from Headline or Terry Pratchett's latest, *Wyrd Sisters*, from Gollancz. One way to find out information about the latest horror and SF books and films is to join The British Fantasy Society. Formed in 1971, the society publishes a regular *Newsletter*, containing plenty of listings and reviews; *Dark Horizons*, a mix of fiction and articles of interest to the membership, plus various one-shot periodicals. The BFS also organises the annual *Fantasycon*, which attracts some of the top names in the field, and presents the annual British Fantasy Awards for excellence in the genre. Membership is open to everyone and costs £10 per annum in the UK or $24 in the US (including air mail postage). For more details send a stamp addressed envelope to: The British Fantasy Society, 15 Stanley Road, Morden, Surrey SM4 5DE, England. And remember to tell them *Fantasy Tales* sent you.

The Cauldron is essentially a letters column where we let our readers air their views on the magazine and its contents and choose their favourite stories. We would like to reiterate that your comments will be much appreciated, so keep sending us those letters! Now, without further delay, let's see what some of our readers thought about our tenth anniversary number...

The
BRITISH FANTASY
Society

The **British Fantasy Society** was formed in 1971 to provide the discerning reader with a greater coverage of the fantasy, science fiction and horror fields. To achieve this, the Society publishes a *Newsletter,* packed with information — news and reviews of the numerous films, books and magazines that confront the fantasy fan. Besides the *Newsletter,* the **BFS** also publishes a number of other magazines, notably *Dark Horizons,* the Society's journal containing fiction and articles, the fiction periodical *Winter Chills,* and the *Masters of Fantasy* series.

In addition to publishing magazines, the **BFS** organises an annual **Fantasy Conference** which attracts many of the top names in the field. At these events the **British Fantasy Awards** are presented for categories such as Best Novel, Film and Short Story. Amongst those who have enjoyed the benefits of the Society are:

Piers Anthony, Clive Barker, Ken Bulmer, Ramsey Campbell, Adrian Cole, Stephen Donaldson, Dennis Etchison, Stephen Gallagher, Charles L. Grant, M. John Harrison, Robert Holdstock, Diana Wynne Jones, Stephen King, Dean R. Koontz, David Langford, Tanith Lee, Fritz Leiber, Brian Lumley, George R.R. Martin, Michael Moorcock, Peter Straub Peter Tremayne, Lisa Tuttle, Karl Edward Wagner, Manly Wade Wellman, Gene Wolfe. . .

British Fantasy Society membership is open to *everyone.* The U.K. subscription is only £10.00 pa; $24.00 in the U.S.A.; £13.00 in Europe and £18.00 elsewhere (Sterling and U.S. funds only please). Make your cheques or money orders payable to the **British Fantasy Society** and send them to the Society's secretary:
Di Wathen, 15 Stanley Road, Morden, Surrey, SM4 5DE, U.K.

Ⓗ

Not a Bad Tale

Regular *FT* illustrator Alan Hunter writes from Boscombe East, Bournemouth: "Many thanks for the tenth anniversary issue of *Fantasy Tales* (has it *really* been that long?) Comparing it with issue 1, although the basic format has remained unchanged, there has been an obvious improvement in every department—more pages, neater typeface, full-colour covers, more varied layout with full-page illustrations and half-tones etc. There is also a noticeable swing away from the heroic fantasy tale towards the dark fantasy and horror story, but if this is an improvement depends on whether this is a response to readers' demands or because you are not having much good heroic fantasy material submitted.

Assessing the stories in this issue is difficult, as usual, because there is not a bad tale among them. Even after careful consideration I am left with the problem of how to allocate three places to four stories.

In first place I nominate *The Travelling Salesman and the Farmer's Daughter*. C. Bruce Hunter (I hesitated using his name in case I am accused of bias) leads the reader gently and persuasively through to the fantastic climax. My second choice may not be generally popular because the descriptions and dialogue read like a 1930s film script. I am sure this is deliberate and I command Mike Chinn for an original approach to the horror story in *The Hollywood Mandate*. Now comes my dilemma of wishing to shoe-horn both *Writer's Curse* and *Ghoul of the Four Winds* into third place. Although Ramsey Campbell displays his usual mastery of the telling phrase, William Webb's unusual story lingers longer in the mind, so I will choose that for third.

The remaining items, although competent, are basically padded anecdotes. Like the poetry, they serve very well to provide variety to the magazine's contents, but are impossible to judge alongside fully-rounded stories. However, they are all still enjoyable in their own right."

Many Happy Returns

From Edgware, Middlesex, Simon MacCulloch sends his congratulations: "Many happy returns on *FT*'s glorious tenth. I didn't think I was going to need to dust off my sunglasses this summer until issue 17 emerged from its modest buff envelope. The spear-tip intersecting with the logo was a nice touch to note after my retina had recovered from the shock. The fiction opened in similarly sparkling form. *The Dandelion Chronicles* is probably the funniest spoof I've ever read—it's been a while since I had the impulse to laugh aloud at anything in print other than an election manifesto, and only the fact that I was sitting on a crowded underground train at the time stopped me from doing so in this case, reducing me to a kind of soft choking sound that proved equally embarrassing . A firm first choice.

Ramsey Campbell's *Writer's Curse* is equally secure in second place, an interesting variation on his EC Comics-inspired tales, justifiably rescued from obscurity.

Third place could go to any of several stories, but I found Mike Chinn's *The Hollywood Mandate* the most consistently entertaining of the remainder. A dud, I'm afraid, was present in the form of *Hell is a Personal Place*. I think Brian Lumley is a fine writer, but I found this particular story trite. Now that I've said this it will probably be voted best story. So it goes.

Nice to see that there's yet more vividly expressed reasons for topping ourselves to be gleaned from the Robert E. Howard legacy. However, my own favourite among the poems was *Ebony Rose*, probably because I didn't quite understand it.

So there we are. My advice for the next ten years would be keep up the standards, keep up the traditions, and keep down the price!"

Record to be Proud of

Dave Reeder writes from Malfort Road, London: "What, ten years? Already? In a world of magazine editors who produce two or three issues and then vanish (my own name comes uncomfortably to mind!) the work of the Jones/Sutton hybrid is astounding. Not only has *FT* introduced me to a great number of authors who have enriched the fantasy/horror scene, it has also reintroduced us to a number of major figures sadly neglected for many years. A record to be proud of.

Of course, the years have taken their toll—I know I am not the only one to regret profoundly the fact that Manly Wade Wellman is no longer with us. However, the rise of new talented authors will ensure that the world of fantasy fiction continues to grow and I hope that *FT* continues to grow and reflect the changes.

So, well done and thank you for 17 enjoyable issues. Thank you too for managing to create a semi-informal grouping of authors, artists and editors whose meetings at conventions and parties have done much to cement relationships—it would be presumptuous to talk of an *FT* school but an *FT* circle of friends seems reasonable.

Criticisms: well, I can't be alone in wondering when you are going to exclude yourselves from the self-confessed embarrassment of winning yet another British Fantasy Award, despite such awards being deserved. What else? We could look at *FT* 17, of course, which I found to be amongst the weakest ever. Shame that, but still streets ahead of so much on the market. Favourite stories—Nolan, Hunter, Campbell."

Fantasy Celebration

From Marlborough, Wiltshire, Ian Mundell tells us: "Many thanks for *FT* 17, and many happy returns for your 10th year.

It strikes me as strange that with such a range of 'big name' writers in the issue, there was a good deal of fiction about other writers present: William F. Nolan sent up Ray Bradbury (which upset me a little since his fiction is as much a part of my childhood as the mid-west was a part of Bradbury's); Michael Moorcock sent himself up (no-one does it better), and Ramsey Campbell took a swing at the profession in general. The field of fantasy celebrates itself again, which I suppose is only appropriate.

Favourite this issue was C. Bruce Hunter's *The Travelling Salesman and the Farmer's Daughter*—despite the slight fumbling towards the end the beautiful final image wasn't marred. It's the sort of touch I admire in Ray Bradbury's stories, and an object lesson to the pedlars of purple prose and overkill writing.

Second comes Ramsey Campbell's *Writer's Curse* for its superb execution and its sense of humour. We expect nothing less from the man. Third is *The Ghoul of the Four Winds* by William Thomas Webb for originality and its traditional 'English' flavour. Favourite illustrations were Stephen Fabian's cover and Martin

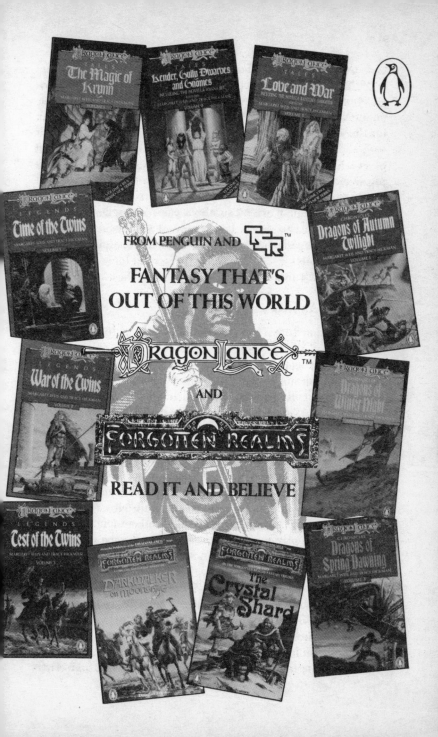

McKenna's interior for *The Hollywood Mandate*.

Of the other fiction, I appreciated Michael Moorcock's Eternal Champion joke, but found Brian Lumley's piece a little inconsequential. It reminded me of an illustration by Stephen Laurence for the 1945 Joe Archibald story *Heaven Only Knows*. I didn't have the story to compare it with, but the picture has the Angel of Death, Fuehrer, fields of dead etc.—so the whole idea struck me as familiar. Mike Chinn's *The Hollywood Mandate* was just too over the top: if it was serious there were too many clichés; if it was a send-up it wasn't subtle or camp enough—no need to beat the subject to death. It was nice to see the return of the Golem, though. All of the poetry was enjoyable, although nothing was exceptional.

Thanks for another good issue."

Lacklustre Anniversary Issue

Peter Tennant from Thetford, Norfolk, takes us to task: "Some comments on *Fantasy Tales* 17, an issue that I found regrettably lacklustre, especially so given its tenth anniversary status. I think possibly the desire to cram in famous name writers over-ruled your usual excellent judgement.

As a Bradbury fan I was rather wary of a parody by someone whose main claim to fame is *Logan's Run*, and rightly so as William F. Nolan's feeble offering proved. There is a lot of silliness in Bradbury's work, but such is his skill as a writer that the credibility gap is breached. On the other hand, Nolan can't even make silliness work as silliness. He piles oddity on oddity in a manner never funny and ultimately tiresome. Great writers can and should be parodied, but only by those of comparable ability. Lesser talents only underline their own inadequacy.

Someday I mean to pick up a novel by Ramsey Campbell and find out what all the fuss is about. *Writer's Curse* was a competent piece, but nothing special. No depth to the characterisation, no sense of atmosphere, no great inventiveness to the plot. A mere space filler.

More padding in *The Last Call*. As an avid reader of the Eternal Champion cycle I feel cheated, insulted even, at this cheap end to an honourable tradition (though in retrospect, given the

wry humour that permeates Moorcock's work and his fondness for puncturing balloons, perhaps this ending was not wholly inappropriate).

The Travelling Salesman and the Farmer's Daughter was one of the issue's better offerings, giving a neat twist to the old joke. C. Bruce Hunter knows how to pace a story, how to create believable characters and situations. My only complaint is that the ending was rather an anticlimax. It should have been more horrific and arisen naturally out of events not, as it seemed to me, just tagged on.

The evil of Hitler and the Nazis has been done to death by now, and *Hell is a Personal Place* by Brian Lumley added nothing new to the theme. A competent but uninspiring space-filler, the quality of the writing offset by the unoriginality of the thought.

The style of *The Hollywood Mandate* attempted to recapture the suspense of those old Saturday matinée cliffhangers, right down to the corny nomenclature of Damien Paladin. It came as no surprise to learn that Mike Chinn writes for comics, where such standards still hold by the very nature of the medium. For me it worked only as nostalgia, a reminder of how naïve we once were to take such things seriously. On reflection I suppose I enjoyed it, but not much.

The Ghoul of the Four Winds had a nice feel to it, putting the time-honoured tradition of the evil clergyman to good use and shunning a more conventional happy ending in favour of the bittersweet. Kudos to William Thomas Webb on an original and evocative piece of fiction.

Six Commonplaces was atrocious. I can't believe you printed it for any other reason than to have Clive Barker's name on the cover. The remaining poetry shone by comparison but was unremarkable in its own right. Artwork too was below par, with no single piece that was really striking or memorable.

To survive ten years is a real achievement, but you'll have to do better if you expect to see out another ten. Not to worry though, the quality of issue 16 has me convinced you can do it."

The Best Yet

Peter Bayliss writes from Street Ashton, Rugby: "Congratulations on *FT*17, the best yet and a very worthy issue to celebrate ten years of publication. In fact, there were so many good stories that it became difficult to sort out three in order of preference.

However, William F. Nolan's *The Dandelion Chronicles* was my first choice. I thought this was a brilliant pastiche of Bradbury's style. Didn't someone once say imitation was the sincerest form of flattery? My second choice was Moorcock's *The Last Call*, reminiscent of his comical 'self-parody' *The Stone Thing* in *FT*1. He admits in his introduction to *Wizardry and Wild Romance: A Study of Epic Fantasy* that he's "unable to muster much nostalgic response to old pulp magazines." I suspect all his writing in the fantasy genre is to be taken with a large pinch of salt. My third choice was a split between Lumley's *Hell is a Personal Place* and Ramsey Campbell's *Writer's Curse*.

Runners-up were C. Bruce Hunter's sensual tale *The Travelling Salesman and the Farmer's Daughter* and *The Ghoul of the Four Winds* by William Thomas Webb. Although Hunter's short pieces in *FT*12 and 14 were very good, this one was a welcome return to the longer yarn as in *To Welcome One of Their Own* in *FT*11 where he could build up the atmosphere. And I thought Webb's story a big improvement on *The Hypnocosm* in *FT*2.

The artwork in this issue was excellent, especially the 'odorous Irish beggars' by Jim Pitts, and Nicholson's illustration for *The Last Call*. And I think Fabian's front cover by itself deserved to make *FT*17 a bestseller. Of course, it didn't illustrate any of the stories, but who's complaining?"

Your Favourite Story

According to the readers, the best story in *Fantasy Tales* 17 was William F. Nolan's pastiche of Ray Bradbury's tales, *The Dandelion Chronicles*. It was followed by a tie in second place between Ramsey Campbell's *Writer's Curse* and *The Travelling Salesman and the Farmer's Daughter* by C. Bruce Hunter. Please remember to let us know which three stories you enjoyed most in this issue, and send your votes to: Fantasy Tales, 11 Shepherd House, Shepherd Street, London W1Y 7LD, England.

Cover Artist—Chris Achilleos

This issue's cover is by leading science fiction and fantasy artist Chris (Christos) Achilleos. Recognized as one of the most accomplished illustrators working in Britain, to date he has published three acclaimed books of his work: Beauty and the Beast, Sirens *and, most recently,* Medusa *(Dragon's World, £14.95 hardcover; £7.95 paperback). One of the more bizarre aspects of the immense popularity of Chris's work is that his illustrations are copied as tattoosmore frequently than any other artist.*

His first real encounter with fantasy was in 1967, while he was attending art college. He came across a copy of Robert E. Howard's Conan the Conqueror *in a second-hand bookshop, and the cover by Frank Frazetta caught his eye. For Chris this was something new. He was already interested in fantasy, but his knowledge was limted to the classical legends of the Ancient Greeks and Romans.*

Conan's colourful adventures came as a revelation to the young artist: "You are transported to a galaxy far, far away. There are warriors, empires, wizards, black magic and monsters," he explains. "You are not sure where it is, but it's great to be there."

For Chris, Conan symbolises the free spirit of man. He believes human society is at its most stable when man lives the simple, uncomplicated life of a hunter-gatherer or nomad. Such societies, like those of the North American Indians, survive for thousands of years in tranquility with nature. Civilisation, while it produces great achievements, is an ever-spiralling force whose benefits all have human and environmental costs and which today is looking increasingly out of control.

Chris feels that he owes his success to being in the right place at the right time. In the late 1960s and early '70s, fantasy and science fiction books flooded into Britain from America. The market was booming—thanks to Tolkien, Howard and Lovecraft—and they needed cover illustrations, particularly as the standard of artwork was often not very high. He got his first commission by brazenly phoning the art director of a

102

publishing company and informing him he could do better!

He got the job and since then has done cover illustrations for countless books, particularly such series as Dr. Who, Star Trek, Robert E. Howard and, one of his own favourites, Michael Moorcock. He has also worked extensively with Ian Livingstone of Fighting Fantasy fame, producing covers both for the game books and White Dwarf magazine.

More recently, Chris has become involved in the movie world, working on a wide variety of films including the costume and conceptual designs for George Lucas's epic fantasy adventure Willow. He particularly enjoys the scope of such work—the opportunity to visualise entire worlds—and hopes that he will become increasingly involved in such projects.

However, for the time being, we'd like to welcome Chris to the pages of Fantasy Tales, and look forward to seeing his work grace the covers of future issues of the magazine . . .

interzone

SCIENCE FICTION AND FANTASY